NIHARIKA NIGAM

Published by
Invincible Publishers
201A, SAS Tower, Sector 38, Gurugram – 122003
Phone: +91-124-4034247, +91 9599667779
www.invinciblepublishers.com

Sales: Office No. 109 Prakash Mahal
Ansari Road Daryaganj,
Near ICICI Bank - 110002
Phone: +91-11-40198405
Email: invinciblepublishers@gmail.com

First edition – 2022

Title: 3...2...1... JUMP
ISBN: 978-93-94200-34-0

To Papa,

For my wings.

To Mom,

For being the relentless wind underneath them.

Acknowledgements

Whoever knew it takes a village and a half to put together rambles of thoughts into one cohesive story! After over a year of pouring into this, of editors and beta readers and publishers joining the mix, I finally had something I loved.

Writing is neither linear nor pretty. But there are those that rub in neither and go about their days like you're not behaving like a zombie with a brain freeze. To my parents, you deserve all the credit for everything I will ever accomplish. You know my love of writing only exists because of your joy in reading it.

My editor, Dagny. Oh, you had me at hello. Literally! Our email exchange would probably deserve a book of its own. She did the unthinkable and made me fall in love with editors. Or maybe (and most likely) just with her. To have added so much to the book without changing a thing about my thoughts or my style of expression is some weird kind of magic.

To all the teachers that scribble little notes of encouragement in the margins of students' answer sheets—you may not know it, but you shape our dreams.

Finally, I have to thank my publisher, Invincible Publishers, for having faith and backing me like a team that's…well, invincible.

Introduction

Witnessing the journey of pioneering a brand new adventure into the Indian market has been just as exciting as standing at the literal edge.

The relationship between the jumper and the Jump Master is a special one. Right on the edge and just before the free fall. It is where the seeker meets the sought, the fears meet the courage, and the questions...well, they find perspective. In that sense, it always reminded me of Krishna and Arjun as they stood at the brink of war, bonded by their journey, spearheaded by the warrior and backed by the teacher.

It was a landmark for adventure tourism in the country when we hit 1 lakh jumps in 2020. But why is that something to celebrate?

Because in those one lakh jumps, every single bungy has had a story to tell. A story of fears and of the courage to overcome them. A story like this.

This particular one is a little about me, a little about you—and a lot about our time.

1

Can't wait to experience the world again?

We've got something you can hold onto!

Send us your story and why daring to take the last step off the edge is just what you need, and we'll gift you the experience of a lifetime:

INDIA'S HIGHEST BUNGY!

In Rishikesh!

NANKI ran her fingers through her hair, as she often did when something caught her fancy in a distracted moment, subconsciously bracing herself to pay attention. A broken Dorito fell out.

'What even...?' She whispered into the darkness, from under her blanket, momentarily distracted from her distraction. She hadn't even had a Dorito today.

Was it yesterday? Wait, what time *is it?*

But before she could trace back to the exact moment that this chip and her life crossed paths, the video post on Instagram had hijacked her attention back onto the screen.

This foreign-looking man with salty-looking hair, a dirty brown colour that curled carelessly at the edges, a mischievous twinkle in his eye, looked into the camera and out at her before edging towards jumping off what looked like a yellow bridge with ankle straps tied to a rubber chord. He raised his eyebrows, his eyes widened, and his face stretched as if to say 'eeeeeep... I can't believe I'm doing this!'

As he threw his arms out like a bird and bungy jumped, he looked so deliriously excited to be *alive.*

It was an emotion she remembered… and missed.

Nanki rubbed her tired eyes, put on her earphones and watched it again.

And again. With the sound on, she could now hear the wind gush wildly as a faint countdown erupted in the background: "3…2…1.. JUMP!" right before his shrill shriek tore through and he dived, full out, high on life.

She went back to the post.

'Can't wait to experience the world again?'

She reread it thrice. Before she knew why, she broke down—silently.

With tears coming down faster than rain, Nanki was properly sobbing. Sometimes things divide life into a before and an after. It had been like a train wreck since.

The pandemic had been waging for a whole year, with bad months and worse ones. Far worse than anything anyone had anticipated.

It had been a period of grave tension between clinging desperately to a sense of safety and control while witnessing death, loss and helplessness on a daily basis.

With Delhi running out of oxygen and hospital beds, there was a constant anxiety that dragged on long enough to turn into a paranoia that was now hard to switch off.

But *still.* This was a whole new level of insanity.

Must be going nuts, she thought. Who cries at a Bungy advertisement?

And yet, it felt cathartic. She *missed* the world so much, it hurt.

She missed the infectious energy of a crowd. She missed hugging friends. She missed chasing the sun as Dhruv took her on endless drives with no destination. She missed the aunty she sat opposite and smiled at on the metro every day. She wished she had asked her name. She missed travelling to new places and truly experiencing the world.

And it *ached* to see everything fall apart. She ached for her neighbour, for the people who died gasping for air, for togetherness.

For health, for abundance.

For the joy of being alive.

For the warmth found in a cafe.

This was her life, her world, and there was no sugar-coating it: it was *dying.*

Silently that night, Nanki stole a moment to grieve.

She grieved for people she had never met and for places she had never been to.

Most of all, she grieved for time that was lost.

***

The day had been weird. But it was a time when weird was normal, and so she guessed, it was a normally weird day.

Nanki, having to deal with the human resources team, realised that resuming regular life after the pandemic was not going to be easy. They had wanted employees to start resuming office three days a week. While Nanki had been waiting to get back, now that the option actually presented itself, she felt a nagging paranoia creep up, making it hard to accept. It was an argument that she ended by citing her living with her aged grandfather. Not that Covid-19 had spared the younger generation.

In all honesty, there was no rationality to systemising this chaos. Like the three-days-a-week schedule.

Did the virus hibernate on alternate days?

She was currently working on rebranding a sports beverage that aimed to 'give people just the energy boost they needed'.

As if, she had thought frustrated, sitting on her sofa, her long slender legs curled under her. She wore her loose white tee and brick red cotton Patiala pants, staring at her laptop. She was working from home during yet another lockdown announced in the city. This was the fourth day she hadn't washed her hair and it showed despite the messy bun that usually hid it well.

There was nothing subtle about milking the cow of this ravaging sickness to increase sales. It felt opportunistic and wrong—mainly because it was. She was glaringly aware of her role in it but well, she had bills to pay and morality didn't come cheap.

Not right now when she was only getting fifty percent of her salary anyway for who knew how long. So she bit her lip, discarded the privileged brand of righteousness she couldn't afford anymore, swallowed her curses and clung on.

Dhruv, her husband of four years, had been in charge of dinner today. This meant he had spent a majority of the evening on YouTube, searching for a fancy recipe in his room.

They'd worked out an alternate day cooking system between the both of them for the week, since staff wasn't allowed into the building. Over the weekends, Nanu, her maternal grandfather, would choose the menu and they'd cook together with music in the background. He had been living with them since her parents had announced that they wanted to relocate to Ooty to live out their retirement plans, a year after their wedding. Nanu had been too old to uproot and replant. While it was never forced upon them, Nanki and Dhruv had moved into his space to look after him and made it their first marital home.

It was a good system.

Food accounted for. Equality accounted for. A pocket of happiness accounted for.

Check. Check. Check.

Work wise, however, her system hadn't been doing so well.

There had been a growing dissonance between her job and her *working*.

Nanki had usually loved the creativity of bringing brands to life.

She was bold in her designing. Her boss Jaya called her the 'go big, or go home kind-of-girl' and entrusted her with brands that were comfortable with taking risks and stepping outside the box.

She would take mere retail products and make them come alive with emotion by weaving them into compelling stories. She gave them a personality that was larger than life. She went for *aspirational* rather than inspirational.

The star performer on her team, she effortlessly wowed her customers, which is how she landed this project.

However, of late, she was slacking. Not in the least in terms of time. In fact, working from home seemed to have blurred all boundaries between working hours and home time.

Layman and Associates would—and did—call her at any time and she was expected to answer because 'it's not like you have to be in office'.

Oh, but I AM Jeff. My whole life is now the office.

Jeff from their Singapore office, was part of the Layman and Associates team working on this beverage. The beverage company was trying to relaunch it in the South-Asian market within the next quarter.

He was exhausting in general, but had never been this uncouth.

By about nine pm, when this remark was thrown at her over her umpteenth work call that day, she had been staring at the laptop, starving, while scanning twitter for a hospital bed for her twenty-year-old neighbour's mother who needed a ventilator. At her elbow, her third cup of chai had gone cold.

She had wanted to punch him in the face, but instead, rolled her eyes, contained her muttering under her breath, and answered politely, "I'll send over the new theme options by midnight."

Urgh, adulting.

***

As Nanki lay awake at a quarter past one now, having shared the drafts she knew were average and banging her laptop shut, not caring anymore what Jeff thought of it, she wondered if her neighbour had found a bed.

Dhruv was asleep next to her, satisfied from having whipped up an excellent Tomato Pulao. She could hear Nanu cough through his sleep in the other room.

She hated being average. She hated being called out on it. And yet, she was finding it increasingly difficult to bring that… *life force* out of her, needed to function well.

A weird kind of fog seemed to have settled upon her brain. Some days it felt like the world was crumbling around her and all she could do was keep her head low and scroll through Instagram till the nightmare was over.

That's how she arrived here today, unprepared, at this bouquet of emotions suddenly in full bloom in the middle of the night.

Rishikesh! she read the post again.

She remembered visiting it often with her family as a child. It felt familiar and comfortable to look at it now. The mountains behind the jumper, the sound of the wind… they transported her back.

Mum would sit with her cup of chai by the Ganges and Dad would love taking their pictures.

Some days, they'd go rafting in the rapids of the Ganga and return home all wet from the chill waters of the holy river.

And oh, the *pahadi khaana*—how much she missed it now! Cooked with locally grown vegetables and sinfully greasy.

The warming camp bonfires were a comfortable memory and she felt a sudden pang to go back to the old—but this time to think anew.

She wanted to do everything she hadn't done here before. Be everyone she could have been. Build different from the same bricks. Create fresh from the same roots.

Maybe then it might all end differently.

And that's why that night she responded. And that's how she met him.

2

I want to consume those mountains

and inhale them until they fill me up

and nothing else remains.

ONE line was all she wrote, never expecting to hear back. No one responds to random Insta DMs anyway.

She just wanted to touch Rishikesh and write an ode to the mountains, the mood that she was in that night.

But within minutes, she saw three dots light up and down.

This random stranger, with clearly nothing better to do that night, was responding!

You'd need a really big appetite for that! *mischievous grin emoji*

Oops. There was a person on the other side of this phone. Nanki suddenly felt embarrassed.

Oh, haha!

I only meant I want to consume the mountains

like you do as you dive into them,

while I still have the chance

and while they still stand there,

unchanging and majestic.

She imagined him sitting in the heart of the mountains, as if he lived on that bungy bridge.

The messages weren't yet seen.

She checked his profile. It was the official page of the bungy place—Jumpin Heights.

The bio read: 'This is where you meet your fears. Got Guts??'

What an interesting living, Nanki thought.

1 new notification

The stranger had responded with a picture. It was blurred for privacy sake and she wondered if she should open it.

Oh well, it's a brand page. Couldn't be unsolicited pictures of the human anatomy. *Or could it?*

She checked the time. It was almost two am now. Carefully, suspiciously, she opened it.

It was a live picture, almost pitch black. In the distance however, she could see the faint silhouette of the Garhwali peaks, the foothills of the Himalayas.

The mountains, right now.

Below it, he had written:

When this is all over,

they will be right here, waiting.

Unchanging and Majestic.

A love letter written in blood could not have meant more. She stared at the picture, took a deep breath in and shut her eyes, to burn the image in, as if to lock it safe within her.

After a minute, she hearted the picture, because there was nothing really she could say, but smile a smile that was far more complex in its emotional depth than the one she could send through emojis.

"Pahaadon ki sardiyaan, aur kulhad waali chai. Bass aur kya? (The cold of the mountains and tea in an earthen cup. What else is life?)" her father would have declared as a life motto, to a view like that. Remembering his deep, big voice now made her feel safe and warm.

Before she dozed off to those memories, she zoomed into the mountains again, and realised that if she looked closely enough, she could almost hear them breathe.

***

The next morning, Nanki woke up to Dhruv nudging her.

"Morning sunshiiiine."

She sleepily protested, at what she knew was coming. He hugged her before whispering "Breakfast is your turn today!" and with an evil laugh, walked into his study.

She half smiled, half rolled her eyes, and got out of bed to resume what seemed like an endless day, broken only by a few naps and a couple of daydreams.

***

The next couple of days came in like a hurricane.

Kavya, her next door neighbour, had not yet found a bed for her mother when her father was diagnosed as Covid-positive too and declared critical. Had this been a movie, Nanki noted wryly how Dhruv would have laughed at how bad the script was, except it wasn't.

It was a nightmare alright, but it was real: terror walked amongst us.

Little Kavya. Barely out of her teens and the older of two siblings. At a time when neighbours had no reason to talk to each other, hers was the only family on the street they actually had a relationship with. The only ones they sent Diwali sweets over to, shared food with.

As Nanki found herself assimilating the jenga blocks of their relationship, as if to brace herself for impact, she realised how exquisitely rudimentary it was—like the most basic of human instincts and yet—or maybe that *is* why—it was her only sense of community amidst an otherwise concrete jungle.

Nanki couldn't imagine an entire familial unit breaking down like this. Least of all *them*.

Little Kavya, who had gone running to the medical store to get her medicines when Nanki was down with a viral and Dhruv was travelling on work. She had bought her an extra pack of chocolate biscuits that day just because. Nanki remembered how she had felt back then. She wasn't a fan of chocolate, had never been. More of an orange cream biscuit kind of person if at all. But Kavya didn't know that. So she bought the next best thing—her own favourite flavour. Somehow Nanki loved that even more.

Little Kavya who always saved her a piece of her birthday cake, even when she was too busy to attend. Again, always chocolate.

Little Kavya, not being allowed to be so little anymore.

Nope. Nanki stopped her train of thought before it prematurely started to accept the worst. *Not going to think it.* Let's just find a bed for now. What if I invite misery in? Isn't that The Secret or Law of attraction or whatever? She asked herself.

An ominous little voice creeped up, engaging in dialogue with her own inside her head: Well then, we're all doomed.

She knew what it meant. With all the papers, the social media, the news there was no escaping the fear. If the fear set in, there was no escaping the possibility…

Dhruv was on call with yet another hospital. His father was a renowned surgeon and they were trying to pull all the strings possible.

No vacancy.

Nanki was sitting at the edge of her seat, barely able to eat. Jeff was texting her furiously, insisting she join the conference call with the client in an hour.

They had just collated some data from their recent sales in the Middle East and wanted to highlight their estimated causes for the 7% jump in sales there.

Nanki could not care less. Not a wee bit—minus one.

This was so ridiculously unimportant that right in this moment she didn't care if she was unemployed for the rest of her life.

She let his calls ring out and wondered what would happen if she just ghosted him and the rest of the company forever, starting now.

She couldn't even put the phone on silent. What if a hospital or lead got back with a vacancy?

As Dhruv continued to make call after call, she kept refreshing the local hospital databases on twitter and telegram for absolutely any relief. She had put out urgent requests everywhere. There were so many people responding to requests, with such a barrage of information that sent her on one wild goose chase after another, leading nowhere. All unverified and outdated sources.

Her phone rang again. She jerked toward it, hoping to hear from their doctor fraternity.

It was Jaya, her boss. Nanki rolled her eyes.

JEFF, the RAT! Nanki muttered malevolently. Complaining to the head mistress like we're in school! Absolute worst of humanity, scum of the earth, may he rot in…

Nope. She couldn't do that anymore; not to her worst enemy, not when it could be true.

URGHHHHH!

Her brain had checkmated her in her imagined fight against this silly little man.

He knew she would never leave Jaya hanging and that's why he played this card.

"Hello" Nanki took a deep breath in to calm herself down.

"Nanki you've been unavailable. You're needed in the meeting in twenty minutes."

Jaya was the human version of an official text.

Nanki pursed her lips, nodded her head in resignation and said after a deliberately audible sigh, "Yes Jaya."

"Good girl!" Jaya said, with the hint of warmth that dripped slowly like golden honey and in doing so, made it even more precious. That was her way of conveying a virtual hug, without indulging her issues, as if already knowing of them and yet nudging her onward to plough through anyway, as if to say, 'March on, soldier'.

And she did.

She respected her too much to refuse.

***

They made jokes about Jaya being her work mom. Simple, stout and formidable, late-fifty-something Jaya. In her crisp cotton sari and big red bindi, Jaya had recruited her right out of college, as a lanky third year student with her hair streaked red and the white canvas sports shoes that were all the rage in Delhi University at the time. She had mentored her into not just being the professional she was today (*usually*, her brain quipped), but also the woman she had come to be. It was more than about just building a comfortable life: in empowering Nanki; investing in polishing her; standing behind her and pushing her forward, Jaya had gifted her an inherent sense of confidence and self-esteem. For that, she would forever be indebted. And so, Nanki found a way to accommodate this one meeting into her otherwise nerve-wracking day, concealing her anxiety under a peach lipstick and a careless swipe of kohl.

***

Dhruv's phone rang at three am. Nanki awoke with a start. Maybe it was a dream or the uneasiness of the day, but she woke up with her heart racing and an instant shock of foreboding.

This happened often, as a knee-jerk reaction to alarms these days.

Dhruv jerked out of his blanket too and fumbled to reach his mobile, sitting up straight and putting on his glasses as if his sight was imperative to this conversation.

"H-Hello…? Ahaan…? okay… okay!" He reached for a notepad and scribbled something down.

"Thank you so much Sir…. thank you."

His voice was still so full of sleep, but he was excited as he hung up.

"Nanki they have one oxygen concentrator system. Ready to be delivered. They'll set up a unit at home. Just have to email the postal address, doing it now. You call Kavya."

The call had been from one of the foundations they had called earlier in the day.

Nanki dialled Kavya. She picked up so fast like she regularly spent her nights attached to her phone, waiting for it to ring.

"Hi didi?"

The question mark at the end of her hello would echo in Nanki's ears for a long time to come. She was waiting on her to get help.

No, not just waiting, *asking* Nanki for a miracle she had no power to provide.

Like a child must look to God in prayer.

Nanki quietly thanked her stars for she did have some good news to give but what followed was a conversation so devastating that her heart would never mend the same again.

"We have one ventilator. They are coming home to set it up. Dhruv bhaiyya is getting ready, he will handle it. Just stay up."

Kavya burst into tears.

She kept mumbling something amidst a thousand thank yous.

"Kavya? It's going to be okay." Even as she said it, she realised how empty that felt. 'Okay' was a luxury now, and she had no authority to make such claims.

"Didi, should I give it to Mom or Dad?"

There was a long pause, the kind there is when a patient flat-lines and the despair is so absolute that all hope is lost.

How could Nanki answer that question?

How could she protect Kavya from having to make that choice? There was no way out.

Even though she wished she could give her some more years to live like the pampered princess she had been, it was time for her to grow up and make decisions that could have real consequences.

Nanki knew it was the right thing to do and so holding tears back she asked, "What do you think?"

"Okay, so mum of course needed it first, but I th-think we may be too far deep to save her," her voice cracked. It was probably the first time she was admitting this, even to herself.

The tears refused to obey any longer and silently rolled down Nanki's face.

"If we don't get another ventilator soon, I don't want Dad to...." her voice trailed off.

This was supposed to have been good news. All words seemed to have gone out of Nanki. She nodded and hmm'd .

"Does this m-mean I'm letting mum die? Am I really letting my mother die?"

Kavya was getting her words out through haunting wails now.

Little Kavya—all broken.

Nanki would never forgive herself for the words she should have said but that never came to her. Maybe they just did not exist.

There was a certain melancholy so deep that 'cry' was just too darn small for it. At three am on that cold winter night, as Nanki held onto her phone in a cruel silence, she *wept*.

***

About two hours had passed when a van drove into their locality and a couple of men in PPE* kits got out holding a big carton. Perching it carefully between them, they went into Kavya's building.

The oxygen concentrator had arrived.

There was an urgency in their stride and as Nanki looked at them from her balcony, she felt such intense relief wash over her that her knees almost buckled.

Dhruv was downstairs waiting to handle the paperwork upon their return. She looked closer at the van and read the bright hand-painted art sprawled across:

Dharma Foundation

Oxygen Langar #OnWheels

She did a quick google search to check them out. A very basic website revealed a group of turbaned men running this charity full time for a decade. In the Sikh community, a langar was traditionally a free communal kitchen attached to their temple or Gurdwara. Although meant for the hungry, it was usually so rich in flavour and love—that

* Personal protective equipment

it attracted tourists, students and the well-fed alike and no one was ever turned away.

Seva or service was an integral aspect of their faith, which meant to help the community without expectations or returns. Towards that altruistic end, during the pandemic, this organisation had taken their communal distribution drive to the roads to arrange for oxygen to those that were starving of breath.

Nanki paced her balcony, ruminating over this, all sleep having left her system as day and night had merged into one ambiguous hue of restlessness.

To serve for services' sake: the simplest, kindest and most extraordinary of motives.

No exchange needed, because you *can*—no, actually, because you *get to*.

About forty-five minutes passed before the men emerged from the building, and huddled around Dhruv below, leaving a distance of about six feet, discussing something in hushed tones. One of the men looked up and for a fleeting second, Nanki locked eyes with him.

Even though he was a fair distance away, and partially hidden behind the face shield, she could've sworn she saw a fire burning in his eyes as they pierced into hers. Not the kind that erupts into flames consuming everything in sight before dying out, but another distinctive kind—one that is silent, rebellious and resolute.

The kind that *perseveres*.

A fire that sparked an ember within her.

Wow, thought Nanki, bathed in a newfound gratitude. This must be what superheroes feel like, if they existed ...and I guess they do!

She felt so small in that moment that all she could do was stand and stare, in absolute awe of the privilege it was to watch what must be God in motion.

Nanki stood there star struck by this most ordinary man, acting out the simplest of teachings: to just do good.

And look at what that did, she thought—it allowed someone to breathe another day.

Simplicity, if done right, is enough. Who knew?

He and she were seemingly cut from the same fabric and woven of the same threads; and yet in this moment he was infinitely *more* than she had ever been.

He turned away and as the men moved swiftly back into their van, onwards towards probably saving another, Nanki felt a pang of envy at their sheer *movement*. What a privilege it must be to give and feed and provide, and the blessing was truly the givers'—they got to justify their existence as an integral link in the invisible chain that connects us all.

As she saw them drive into the sunrise, she felt full within herself: up to the brim with thankfulness and a singular thought:

How worthy it must be to be human if you can play God, even if only for a second!

Even as one continued to gasp for air, they had just been thrown a lifeboat for another and it was time to grab on tight.

Not knowing what to do next, she let that ember guide her, and it took her into the kitchen.

Although a first for her, she did what people have done since the beginning of time for each other from love. As a show of the first gesture of solidarity ever known to mankind; what neighbourhoods and communities must have been built upon:

She took over some freshly prepared, piping hot food for the family next door.

3

LIKE the cold that is left behind after the fog has lifted, a peculiar disquiet had settled into Nanki's bones by night time, worming its way deeper into the centre of her chest. A thick blanket of icy air seemed to have wrapped itself tightly around her heart. Although she was breathing, it was uncomfortable. Not because of Covid, but because of the ordeal of being alive amidst death.

How do you state that out loud when even *that* was such a luxury to have? A luxury people were scrounging, tugging and dying for?

You don't. You bow your head, say thank you to whatever power is keeping you alive and you breathe.

As she hit the bed exhausted beyond the point of any feeling, she seriously doubted if it would ever entirely leave her now. Much as ivy takes hold of trees, this too was becoming part of her being, feeding on her, breathing with her and growing along with her.

She picked up her phone, escaping into the world of social updates. It was much better viewing someone else's life, than witnessing her own.

Today had been what one might think of as a *good* day, all things considered. *What a time to be alive.*

Ah, if only I could legit climb outside of my body and be anywhere but here, she thought sighing into the emptiness inside of her

Oh, wait! *Anywhere but here,* she repeated the thought to herself. She just remembered something, but her fingers seemed to have beaten her to it. They were already scrolling through her DMs to get to him.

I know this might be weird,

but you've done this before

and it meant so much then,

and if it's possible,

it would mean even more today,

So if it isn't too much to ask for,

can you please just take me to Rishikesh tonight?

Of course, he might never respond. Or he just might.

Until she could know for sure, she could comfortably stay suspended in hope. For now, that was enough to help her get through the night. She didn't even care about the outcome when after twenty minutes, her phone vibrated with a new notification.

'Tap to see blurred content' Instagram announced.

This time, she didn't hesitate and clicked it as soon as it arrived into her inbox.

A burst of colour took over her screen. Rushes of vivid imagery in quick succession made her head spin for a second. She halted, tucked a stray strand of hair behind her ear and gave her brain a second to pick up speed to grasp better.

It was a live video shot from atop a bike, as the rider zipped through the bazaar in the heart of Rishikesh.

Nanki caught dizzying glimpses, as rushes of the narrow bustling street flew by.

Vegetable hawkers, people in colourful sweaters and a few in orange robes, fairy lights and bulbs lighting up the road, Rudraksha beads hanging from every other stall, tall posters of various Gods encased in gaudy gold fabric with tassels almost leaping out of them, and despite the loud VRROOMM of the revving engine, the trance-devotional music permeating everything like a heartbeat.

Ah. She took a deep breath and inhaled Rishikesh in.

She knew where this was—just a turn away from Lakshman Jhula, the suspension bridge across the wild and untamed river, Ganga.

Despite herself, her tired face broke into a smile.

As a child, she would jump up and down over the Lakshman Jhula hoping to buoy over the current of air that apparently made it move to its own special rhythm. Maybe she felt it only because she tried so hard to, but she didn't care. Abandoning all caution like the Ganga below her, she just flowed in perfect harmony, as if a part of some grand orchestra.

This chat was becoming a pocket of comfort. And it was surprising each time.

Today, more than anything it was because he just gifted her a flight of fancy, mentally transporting her to a safer land away from the confines of her bed, no questions asked. She was beyond grateful for she had neither the energy nor the words to explain the why.

Service for services' sake.

thank you stranger. Above and beyond.

She hesitated, then typed:

Also, what's your name?

You're very welcome.

I don't know what you are going through, but it's the least I can do.

Bring you a piece of my world—or maybe just a piece of yours back to you.

And hi there! I'm River.

River! The name played on her lips, sitting just right like the perfect note in a melody.

On a normal day, she would have assumed it to be a fake identity. God knows there was no shortage of that online. But something about this just resonated.

A weird kind of déjà vu fell upon her at being served this name. She could not believe she had gone her entire life not knowing it. But it was here now.

How do you feel familiar to something you have never known before?

As if it was an introduction meant to happen for a name just waiting to be revealed.

Most names and words brought up images in her mind. As a brand strategist she used that to her advantage for visualisation.

His however, brought up sounds, of gurgling, abundant, pristine water.

Just flowing effortlessly, giving life along the way, nourishing everything it touched.

River. What a beautiful, beautiful name.

Why aren't more people called River?

Why isn't everybody?

She clearly needed sleep. But she had managed to find an exit route out of her day, and she wasn't about to give it up.

Hahaha, then I'm not sure anyone would want it anymore.

Humans have a way of wanting what they don't have.

We are quite the odd lot, aren't we?

That we are.

Makes one wonder

if what keeps us ticking is simply our constant yearning.

What a nightmare it would be then,

to have all that we desire.

She had no bandwidth left for random wonderments about existence. She was barely getting by her own. She had had a day of feeling and thinking all too deeply, so right now all she wanted was to splash around the surface. She would process later.

A bungy jumper who's also a philosopher? That must be new.

Nah, not a philosopher.

Just a liver.

As innn... the organ?

Oops, hahah... no!

A LIVER.

Of life.

Is that not a word?

Ummmmmm

No?

Oh?

how come?

It should be!

We need a word for someone who is just being alive

like proactively...

A LIVER!!

Kinda starting to feel like I'm talking to an alien.

Tongue-out emoji

I'm sorry English is not my first language.

I find it hard to connect the dots sometimes.

Nanki read his chat again. Half smiling, she had the inkling that he was going to be wrong about this one.

What a shame though.

The language loses out.

Indeed, it does.

He was right. She suddenly felt hurt at how right he was. She felt a desolate sense of how very incomplete all the dictionaries of the world were without this word—or a word for this.

Any word that did not sound like an organ.

Where are you from?

She was keenly aware that he had not yet asked her name. Somehow, it made her trust him more in giving it, just a stranger though he was.

I come from France.

And I am the Bungy Jump Master here.

Whoa. He clearly didn't have to deal with the Jeffs of the world.

So you sell excitement for a living.

No wonder you've taken up the cause of

THE LIVER for the English language,

as you have in life.

Goodness, gracious me!

His name was River. He was a Bungy Jump Master in the foothills of the Himalayas. He threw people off the edge for money. He unknowingly saved the day by sending random people on the internet a virtual tour of Rishikesh.

She was blown away by what life could also look like on some people. It was beautiful!

Hahaha, I guess I do.

But WHY I do it is because people seem to forget that this is it!

The edge reminds them of that. And me.

Every. Single. Day.

It is a powerful place to be.

And if this is all there is,

Then what else is there to do with life than to live it, all too completely?

Ah...

A liver.

I see it now.

Her eyes were screaming for sleep.

I'm Nanki btw.

Good night River :)

Good night Nanki.

shooting star emoji

As her body refused to function anymore, she let herself surrender to the night.

As one last thing though, she hit the 'follow' button before she switched off.

***

Okay, I'm processing it now.

Nanki stood by her window looking out at the street below. Mahesh, the grocers teenage son from down the street, had come to deliver the week's supplies to the building, as per telephonic orders.

Every Friday, he would leave it down below, outside the gate of the building, to be picked up individually for a contact-less delivery. She had given him a standing order to add a pack of chocolates into Kavya's basket every week.

Kavya's mother had passed away two days after her dad had received the oxygen concentrator. What was most devastating was that by that point, it had come as a relief. Her father on the other hand was doing better. There was no telling how Kavya was doing.

Well, she was surviving. It was as little and as much as that.

Today, Nanki spotted Nutella in the neighbour's basket and grumbled within herself for not having given in to the indulgence herself.

Now she'd have to wait another week. To be robbed of running down the street, looking at exciting junk edibles tempting her from the glass cabinets at Anand grocery poked at her a little extra today.

Anand Grocery was a rudimentary store supplying her childhood indulgences for as long as she could remember. Now, as their gated colony of buildings stayed locked down on account of the Covid-positive patients, including Kavya's father, it was reduced to a cold transactional supplier of rations.

So much of the joy of purchasing was leaning in across the counter to look at the goodies stacked right up to the ceiling like Alice in wonderland. At Lalaji's welcoming smile and insistence on pushing the special offers of the week, while asking how Nanu was keeping. In sliding in the sour candy he knew she loved instead of the last few coins of the change.

But it was more than that.

So much of her sense of abundance came from knowing that it stayed lit up, every day of the week, just round the corner, never running out. She never realised that then of course, but now in its absence, she felt insecure.

As she stared at the Nutella with a longing she had never had to experience before, River's words came back to her: It's the least I can do. Bring you a piece of my world—or maybe just a piece of yours back to you.

A piece of yours back to you.

Yes, she reflected now. Somehow being confined to her own home felt like being caged in. As she gave a wry smile at his unassuming wisdom, she noted how this must mean that so much of *her* lay outside of her.

It must mean that she *belonged* to the world. The realisation came only when she felt so much lesser by being separated from it.

A beautiful, beautiful world that she never even realised how much she was a part of till she couldn't be anymore. It was like a symbiotic relationship in itself—her internal ecosystem and the world outside. There could be no harmony in one when there was chaos raging in another. A very co-dependent relationship it seems to be too…

Nanu coughed violently from the living room, halting her train of thought. Dhruv kept insisting they should get him tested and she could hear him nag inside her head every time she heard that cough.

She kept delaying it waiting for it to pass as the cold she knew it must be.

It wasn't.

She drummed her fingers on the windowsill in frustration and went into the kitchen to make him a hot cup of ginger tea. She didn't want to go through this.

Stupid, *stupid* cold, worrying everyone for no reason. Why isn't it going away already?

Dhruv had suggested isolating him for a couple of days. She had refused. He was old and he needed her.

And she needed *him*.

Dhruv cared so much about Nanu that honestly it was just annoying.

Mostly because she felt obliged to bow down to his concern for him, as if his love carried more weight.

In India, women rarely got to prioritise their maiden families after marriage the way Nanki did. If they were lucky, they got to bring along their individuality—but families were casually expected to be left behind, only to be visited once in a while, as guests do.

If they did even that too often or stayed too long, the stability of their marriage was quick to be put under the scanner for viruses. There was a precarious balance that needed to be maintained so that the neighbours didn't have too much to talk about as they dipped their glucose biscuits into their cups of tea. That seemed to be an integral factor to all of decision-making.

Bagging a man open to inviting his wife's kin into his everyday life and loving them as his own, was then, seen as nothing lesser than a wish upon a falling star.

This made Dhruv a frikkin' unicorn.

Despite her feminist leanings, Nanki hated that she felt grateful.

As she added two spoonful of tea leaves into the pot of boiling water, Dhruv walked in, almost at a trot.

"Nanki, seriously man, do you hear him? We have to get the test done…."

His voice trailed off as he caught her glaring at him through the fumes from the bubbling tea.

A frown sprouted up on his face as his worried expression transitioned into a quizzical look comically fast, wondering what he did wrong.

"Fine" she said rather curtly, before pouring all the tea into her and Nanu's cup, leaving him standing alone to make his own.

***

Now for the rest of the day it was going to niggle at the back of her head.

The front was occupied by a series of meetings, which were as tiresome as they could be. They kept her from obsessing over Nanu's test reports, though.

It was the day after the conversation. A man in a white lab coat had come home in the morning wearing a mask and a face shield to do the swab test.

He would put an earbud up Nanu's nose and another around his mouth, he explained, before proceeding to do it.

Nanu was a champ. He listened to him, offered him water, glanced at Nanki and laughed, as if to say, "Well, if these are the ways of this new world…"

The man opened a plastic bag with fresh sanitised supplies and proceeded with his test.

One earbud was clinically thrust up his nose, far too deep up for comfort and made him retch. Nanki glared.

Why couldn't they be gentler?

The other was swirled around his mouth to collect saliva and was done in a jiffy.

He looked up at them and smiled, putting up his palms to tell them he was okay.

She knew he was trying to calm her and Dhruv down. He was eighty-seven, which meant this could go wrong a thousand ways.

She decided to think about the handful of ways it could be okay. Maybe it was just a regular viral. They *do* still exist, she reminded herself.

Nanu decided to be in his room in self-isolation today, but kept his door open. Neither here nor there, but caught in just a little bit of limbo.

Nanki had made him a mug of tea and let her meetings take over.

Today Jaya was leading the discussions on a Zoom video call.

"....so as you see, we need to shift our target audience from teenagers to the late twenties and early thirties bracket. Increasing our price point will help us achieve that. It may sound counter-intuitive now, but there's a better chance of survival by completely rebranding than rehashing the old product in just prettier packaging."

Jeff interjected. "However, we need to consider how people would take to a new drink at a higher price in times of a recession, when the economy is already reeling. Beverages is not a necessity and a crisis of this scale in fact deems it as a luxury..."

What if the report comes positive? Her brain had another tab open altogether, persistently lit up in the background.

In the meeting however, there were two rounds of a back and forth before someone asked Nanki directly.

"Nanki, what's your take?"

She had been only passively listening so far.

"Um yeah, I think we need to rope in the client to see how they feel about it because it is a big decision. Of course, this wouldn't change the product, just our brand communication around it...."

Her voice drifted as another idea suddenly was born inside her.

"Wait…why don't we market it as a necessity though? Take it down from the luxury beverages category and sell it as an essential lifestyle product towards an energy boost, subtly hinting at mental health fatigue around Covid. If it works, we get to capitalise on the spending power of the working population, while not losing out on the budget buyer."

There was a silence while everyone mulled this over.

She felt sick to her stomach.

"This…. will require very careful planning and execution. If done right, it will be a game changer for this brand." Jeff delivered the verdict carefully.

Jaya seemed tense, "We must get the client in the loop as soon as we have a basic strategy in place."

For two hours after that, they discussed the various ways they could position the brand in this unique way. Somewhere deep inside her body, the tab was still open and it was still glitching. Her heart would start racing every time she thought about *what if…*

What if it is positive? Between a couple of 'hmms' and 'yesses', her mind kept buzzing with a pulsating fear:

Would he be able to make it through this if it is? Unbidden the question trooped in and took up all the available space in her head.

Dhruv walked in, tiptoeing around her since yesterday. "Oyi, do you want to take lunch to Nanu?"

She looked up from her laptop and wondered why he couldn't just do it.

"Meeting," she said pointing to her screen where another member from their Delhi office and another from Singapore were bickering over the budget for one of the marketing campaigns.

He raised his eyebrows, surprised, but mouthed 'Okay' and left the room.

She needed to be doing well here because outside this tiny little space was a world of uncertainty.

That was tougher to deal with.

She just wanted to run so hard from there and that that she caught some speed. An odd energy seemed to have taken charge of her today. Like a woman possessed, she was flying with it.

'....And if the client doesn't mind altering the product composition ever so slightly," Nanki cut in, interrupting Maria's pitch of a hypothetical ad campaign, "we could add a dash of turmeric and say it improves immunity."

There was a pause as everyone absorbed this.

Nanki knew- just *knew*- that this idea was a winner.

The drink was a tropical, orange energy drink. A tiny amount of turmeric would alter neither the colour, nor the taste of the drink—but could potentially change their entire brand communication, and thereby perception.

After all, it's only words…

Her brain was on *fire* today. She didn't know what was spurring her on, but it felt *electric*.

Hey! I think I got my mojo back, she thought.

"Oh my god, yes!" Jeff's low whisper failed to mask his excitement. "The exotically traditional punch to resonate with the urban Indian market. The magical cure to all health ailments—Turmeric! Genius!"

His admiration made her skin crawl. She could hear Nanu cough in the other room. She suppressed a pang of… something.

Something that was new inside of her.

On the one hand, she was finally being herself, doing her thing and acing exactly who she was designed to be.

And on the other, there was what seemed to be a meeker, softer voice emerging—almost like a baby trying to make itself heard. She could tell this voice apart by how it repulsed away from her own.

She tried to make sense of it. As she mindlessly saw the screen erupt in a brand new cacophony brimming with excitement at what this proposition could mean, she sat back, a niggling thought forming at the back of her mind:

How does the room within become too small for my own being?

***

The sun had set a long while ago and Nanki had lost all track of time when Dhruv walked in looking deathly pale.

"Nanu's reports just came in."

Her stomach lurched. Why would he look like this saying *that*?

She knew what was coming before he said it.

"He's Covid-positive."

4

So much of what came after that was a blur.

Dhruv's words kept repeating inside her head while she tried to grasp what had just happened.

How could it be?

How was this even possible?!

Her meeting was still dragging on when she got up and just left without any warning, leaving her laptop open, her screen staring at the blank wall behind her.

Nanu is Covid-positive.

Nanu is Covid-positive.

Nanu is Covid-positive!

Wait, what?

WHAT.

Amidst the flurry of actions that followed, as Nanki was still reeling with the shock, she instinctively ran out of her room, towards Nanu to see how he was doing.

He must've seen her and sensed the foreboding. He stood at the doorway, looking enquiringly.

He saw the look in her eyes and raised up a hand to stop her from coming closer.

"WAIT! Just wait right there. What has happened? Has my report come in?"

Nanki was unable to function right, nor to form words that made sense.

Dhruv broke the news: "Nanu… I-it's positive. You're Covid-positive."

He raised up both his hands as a gesture to calm them down, "Bass. Okay. It's all okay."

He started inching back from them. He made to shut the door. Just before he did, he called out, "You have to be strong beta. I'm okay. Just stay safe."

Saying that, he started receding, continuing to peep out at them till the door clicked into its frame, firmly isolating him inside.

***

Guilt. That was the loudest feeling tonight among all the ones competing—and there were many.

She could have chosen to spend this day with him. He would've been worried himself but his protective instincts must've taken over, like they always did, and he always had to be the brave one so that *she* wasn't scared.

He had deserved better today.

Instead, she had spent the day—and in fact her life, prioritising things that when it counted, just did not matter. As she retraced her day, she realised she chose—she actually *chose* THIS day to be marketing a product that had failed before, capitalising on this fear that she was now drenched in. Instead of spending the day with Nanu, even if from across the doorway, assuring him that they would make it through whatever happened.

That was infinitely more precious and yet looking back now, she had regularly traded it for goals that would never ever compare to another moment of basking in the light of his toothy grin.

What she would give to have that now.

WAS THIS KARMA FOR THAT TURMERIC TIP?

Even her thoughts yelled within her.

Sure, it wasn't the most sensitive, but when had a pinch of turmeric ever hurt anyone?

Time. That is the entire game, isn't it?

Everyone always said it, but my GOD, was it true, she thought.

If I spend a majority of my time, which *basically* means a majority of my day, doing things I barely like, for things the world has told me I should want, where will be there any time left for the things I truly love?

She was caught up inside her head again, figuring out the math of life to dissect where she had gone wrong, and why where she was *felt* wrong.

She thought back to the last time she saw fulfilment on someone's face. Her mind threw up the gleeful picture of River, about to jump, with his hands wide open, welcoming life in.

Tell me again, why do you do what you do?

Swimming in her thoughts, she hadn't even realised when she had gone onto Instagram.

River was online.

Hello to you too!

Why do you do what you do?

She repeated. She *needed* an answer.

And what about doing it makes you feel...right?

Well...

The three dots played for a while on her screen before his answer reached her. She stayed glued to her screen like her life depended on it.

That moment on the edge... You can't afford the questions that don't matter there.

In that moment, you suddenly know the ones that do, the ones worth risking it all for.

It doesn't hold any answers—those come from you. But all the questions find perspective.

Stripped down to your basic instincts, you finally meet yourself....

Basic instincts. The things that matter. Nanki was taking mental notes. She waited for him to write further.

Our measurements are skewed. The edge is proof.

Certain moments ARE longer than others.

They occupy more space in our minds, sometimes so much more, that it just has to expand to accommodate it. Then we call it growth.

Just a moment lived fully can stretch across a lifetime.

But a gazillion spent without consciousness are as good as non-existent.

It is the same as sleeping through time.

So how short or long your life is depends entirely on how you spend your moments.

I love how in the English language you say 'spend' for time.

The language did not miss out this time.

It is true. It is an expense of your most valuable, arguably your ONLY real currency.

So, cheap coins or the rarest gems?

Were your moments today long enough to *be* enough?

Nanki paused and shut her eyes, knowing her answer and not liking it.

We talk about life being too short but if spent right, it really is enough.

It is just right and it is just enough.

In making people bungy, I gift wrap that nugget of information and gift it to them in that experience.

It is something else, to witness it: When people are standing at the edge, there is a fervent energy that rises to the surface.

This is the force of life that drives it, making them realize how much existed there in the first place.

It comes from the fear of letting go and the need to cling on. This is where gratitude is born from. Gratitude for what is.

Then rises the burning desire to dive into the unknown, the quest for thrill, the curiosity to experience something new.

This reveals the excitement there is to be found in the human experience of pursuit—to reach for something, to strive for something.

People often forget that in the stability of well-established routines, and then wonder why daily living feels mundane.

And in the middle, there's faith. Faith to make that journey.

In me, to guide them and in themselves, to overcome the demons inside their own head.

When I bungy jump, I experience this *allll*.

To become aware of myself, my fears, my curiosity, my desire, my oneness with the world, my capabilities, and indeed, my every breath, the beating of every heartbeat—all in the matter of a moment or two, is nothing short of magic.

To give that experience to another is to empower—That's why I do this.

That is why it feels right.

Nanki let it all sink in. In that moment, she really and truly felt like a starving beggar looking in from the outside at someone eating an unlimited buffet. She realized with a jolt that what she was, in fact, starving for, was that kind of *passion*. Without that passion, all of time is a purse full of clinking coins. It may look like a lot—but it isn't really.

Wow.

I have never felt that way.

I don't even know what to say.

Have I done this all wrong? She wondered, feeling terribly about Nanu and her choices, and her time and everything all at once.

Really?

I get to feel that way every day.

Time is such a gift.

Now more than ever we get to realise it

as we see people get robbed of it every single day.

I say we 'get to' because that realisation really is a privilege.

I just hope for you to be aware,

Life can be felt this way too, you know?

I mean. Whoever feels that way, man? Who is really happy about the rigmarole of everyday living?

It's just what you gotta do, isn't it?

This man, by his mere ways of thought, was challenging her worldview entirely.

Actually he had no 'ways'. He just *felt*, and he flowed from there. With the audacity to be free.

But there were rules to living, had he missed the memo?

He was making her question the little boxes and cages within herself that she could suddenly see tying her down. This was an uncomfortable feeling.

But. It's like the world tells you
you should want XYZ to have a successful life.
And then like a horse with blinders on
you start chasing those things.
The right education, an appropriate amount of travel,
a good job, marriage at a decent age, a child before it's too late.
And before you know it,
that's the rest of your life.
When do you get to question what YOU truly want?
If you even want any of those things.
If your joy lies outside
somewhere entirely different?
You spend your youth thinking of happiness as something that exists ahead,
in the future,
and you keep making decisions that you think help get you there.

She was rambling now, more to herself.

In your twenties, you do everything as an investment.
Like if you follow this blueprint, you will find fulfilment *tomorrow*.
That anticipation of happiness- we call it *hope*-
keeps you excited in the moment, and you mistake it for fulfilment

and before you know it,

most of your moments have passed you by,

your youth is on its way out

and you are still none the wiser.

Eventually, you get to the tomorrow

and realise it was all a big scam--

there was never any golden pot of fulfilment

waiting on this side.

In your thirties, then, one has to wonder

what *is* tomorrow

if not a sum of my todays?

So then, what about today?

But then, your decisions have been made

and you've settled into some kind of stability that is just about taking root

and so as not to disturb it, you just live with it,

all passion and joy slowly draining out of you,

resigning to the fate of dragging your feet through the rest of your days.

What an effin' sham!

She was spooking herself out. Her mind was racing furiously; her hands almost shook. She was completely spiralling out of any sense of control.

Why was she here? There was no reason to be. She was born in a golden age. No dictatorship, no oppression, no slavery. She had skipped the worst of history and had started from where all her choices were her own. This generation had evolved to have sprouted metaphoric wings but seemed to have also inherited their cage: life's most basic questions seemed to have remained the same—Who I am?; Why I am; How to be, so I can be happy.

Why didn't she know the answers to these by now?

Nanki, there are as many ways to live as there are people.

Limited stay those that can see but a few templates.

But blind are those who cannot imagine

a world beyond what they can see.

There is a Zen saying,

No snowflake ever falls in the wrong place.

She scrunched up her forehead, trying to place this within context.

Okayyyyy.

What does that mean?

She was trying to grasp all that she could. It was a lot to take in for today, but it was precisely because of the kind of day it had been that she had arrived at these questions.

How you feel is valid.

Your feelings are as real as you are.

Just be careful to detangle your own feelings

from those of a loud, shouting world.

How you feel is exactly how you are meant to be feeling.

Follow the trail,

—Be fierce about following it, don't be afraid,

and then have the courage to follow through.

Just like if you're Bungy Jumping *winky face emoji*

Hmph.

How *did* she feel?

It was bizarre to think that she didn't know how she felt inside of her, outside of the blueprint of life she had inside her head, which came from God knows where, which she spent a lifetime following with blinders on.

But you're right. It is a shouting world.

There is so much noise.

It's inside me now. Everyone else's voices.

So much so that I can't tell my own apart anymore.

How do I listen to what I feel?

Wow, to be thirty-three and be asking strangers on the internet about how to feel—NOT acing this grown-up business, was she?

There is a poem I had written...

'These words we hide behind

The ones we expel from deep within

are merely the cloak we've dressed our thoughts in,

A facade to make emotion presentable.

They reveal but a part -

the face hiding the heart-

and therein lies its greatest sin

Because like almost every human creation,

It is so terribly limited-

our flawed idea of a conversation.

For it is too little and it is too small

Compared to the dialogue of our soul,

Because this energy between us

A language of its own, above all

-That was created by God.

My hope for us is thus:

Let's stay silent a while and finally converse.'

Despite herself, she smiled.

So, you're a poet too now?

The mountains make a poet out of everyone.

...

Do you find the answer to your question here?

Did she? Rethinking life at thirty-three was not going to be easy. But it had to be done.

I think I do...

You listen to yourself the same way

you listen to anyone else.

You simply *ask* first.

I find that all our answers lie in asking the right questions.

Your most important dialogue is going to be the one you have with yourself.

Make it count.

Cut out the noise and crank-up your own internal volume.

And how do you do it?

She felt a surge of affection toward him for helping her sort through her thoughts.

By finding my silence.

Et voila!

5.

THERE comes a point to fear, beyond which exists a unique numbness. Hovering there, was an eerie silence and a quiet alertness: a waiting in the wings for the demons to show up; Nanki lived there now.

Over the next few days, she became accustomed to her perpetual discomfort. It became routine to wake up wondering if they would need a hospital bed today. Sanitising every spoon and every towel going in and out of Nanu's room became as normal as dusting the rest of the house. He was just a door away but so out of reach: they couldn't even share air.

The only thing flowing freely between them was music.

It floated out of his room, every day, letting them know that he was fine. Like the Azaan that rises from a mosque, it threw on a thick blanket of hope inviting them to have faith and hold on.

Of course, they video-called him, but most days he held it awkwardly, showing barely a part of his face, or sometimes a corner of his eye—both eyes, on days they were lucky.

They could tell that his cough seemed to be getting more aggressive.

They also suspected that he had lost his sense of taste when he didn't even care for Nanki's bread pudding that he could never help taking second servings of.

He wasn't an emergency enough to get an oxygen concentrator for yet, so every now and then, if he did feel a shortness while inhaling, he would just have to gulp in air, fumbling in the darkness for a single breath.

This really kept them on edge. What were they supposed to hope for? That he gets sick enough to qualify for treatment? It was painful to hear him gasp.

But it wasn't too often.

Today, there was Kishore Kumar on loop and *pal pal dil ke paas* filled their house with the feeling that Nanki associated with home.

She slumped down into her sofa and allowed herself a smile. It seemed like forever since she had had a reason to. That there was no reason to grieve today felt like a solid enough excuse for the indulgence.

Mindlessly, she opened her phone.

WHY would people subject themselves to simulated fear?

It is awful in here.

River was online right now and she saw him get to her right away, as announced by the three dots.

To overcome it.

Aah. Well played.

So you're saying, it's not so much about fear as it is about courage, isn't it?

That's why people must throw themselves off the bridge to Bungy?

Well, yes, and no.

Of course, the victory at the end of the battle is phenomenal.

You can feel the rejoicing trickle down to the depths of your soul.

And trust me, it IS mental warfare at the edge.

But the part before, the meeting with your own fears IS its own experience.

I've Bungy-jumped for the majority of the last three decades

and got tens of thousands

to experience it for themselves.

Yet, it is like nothing I can put into words.

It holds the power to drown you out

or to propel you into a flight.

The choice is yours.

Mental warfare? Yep, definitely sounds about right. She could vouch for it from experience now.

But it's terrible to have to face fears.

It's worse to live with them.

Mic drop moment. Due silence given.

Then, after a minute—

How do people get the courage to overcome it?

It's not so much a 'get' as it is a *gathering* of courage.

Until you need it, you don't know it exists within you.

Another reminder of our own infinity, isn't it?

Sometimes, we are beyond our own reach.

It is just that under stress, we have to catch up.

The choice is this:

Which part of yourself do you feed?

The fear of the fall or the chance to fly?

This choice becomes a mood and a mood can become your whole personality.

It spills into daily living too: do you shrink down into the safe and familiar?

Or do you dare to go beyond and rise into an unknown?

Shrink down into a safe and familiar or dare to go beyond…

The words hit a chord. She just thought of something.

You know, I just realised.

I might be a thousand kilometres away from your bridge.

Yet I already am at the edge too.

So help me understand it. Because I need to figure out what my choice is, and how to follow through when I do.

All I can tell with certainty is that it too feels like standing on the brink of war.

And you're right about it feeling like mental warfare.

It is.

I figured if you could manage to take me to Rishikesh, you could help me walk down this bridge till I get to the edge too.

You see, there are a ton of questions and much fewer answers.

Since you're such an expert on courage, can you help me gather mine from wherever it exists inside me?

If it does, that is.

At this point, I frankly don't know.

He must think she's crazy. Somehow she didn't care what he thought of her—why would she? She barely knew him. Not in real life anyway. Weirdly enough, that helped.

She wondered why it was easier to be honest with strangers about her internal battles.

Maybe because everyone she knew was in equal suffrage. Or in different kinds of suffering, but rather equally.

How could someone bleeding themselves, bandage the wounds of another? It almost felt selfish to dump her grievances on her own people. She was as empty in helping them, as she knew they would be to her.

Not that he may not have issues of his own, nor that he may not be dealing with this breakdown of the world himself; however, he did seem to be dealing with it *better*.

Besides, she did not know of them, and maybe that's why she could pretend that those burdens were not hers to carry.

Also, maybe because from this distance she could imagine him to be just perfect, in perpetual peace and harmony, having all the answers to every question figured out.

He was the unknown factor, oddly sitting in the middle of a puzzling equation. *Her* puzzling equation.

Assuming a value—any value—to x only helped get closer to the solution.

Even if in the end, x=0.

It was a whole minute before he said anything.

Then—

It's what I am here for :)

It's settled then!

I bring you my fears and you teach me of courage.

She smiled. In a weird way, she felt somewhat secure in knowing that someone out there had her back. Or in this case, the metaphoric rubber chords. She chuckled at the thought.

Deal.

***

First things first.

The next morning, after the talk with River had been slept over, Nanki had to open this conversation. While most of it had to be an internal dialogue, she had to bring along those she was walking this journey with.

"Dhruv," she blinked hard. She wasn't sure what made her so nervous.

She had gone over this conversation over and over in her head last night, and yet it was something she had not yet fully thought through. She could sense this weird energy building up but she hadn't quite figured out the why, how and where of it all.

She knew that, she did; but she had to get it out already.

She also knew that in none of those hypothetical conversations did she sound sane, or convincing, even to herself.

Dhruv looked up from his laptop, his stubble glistening with a few greys. He was awfully quiet these days, buried under a pile of work, keeping to himself.

"I-I don't know. I don't enjoy my work anymore," she blurted in a rush.

"Tch!" He shrugged in agreement like it was the most normal tragedy in the world. "I'm sorry Nan." He turned back to his laptop.

"I mean it!" she said, pushing through.

He looked up again, widening his eyes now.

"Okayy? No one is, not right now." He was looking at her keenly, wondering why she was stating the obvious all of a sudden.

"No, but I mean. It isn't making sense to me anymore." she was dangerously close to breaking down. Again, she wasn't sure why.

"How can we—I…waste … I can't help but question the futility of everything. Of all my choices and my entire life."

He frowned, surprised.

"You're just feeling guilty you couldn't be there for Nanu that day and the days before his isolation because you were occupied by your meetings." His tone was flat and emotionless.

He wasn't wrong.

"So what if I am?" her voice was rising, without permission. She felt frustrated that he couldn't understand the gravity of how she felt.

He looked at her like she was crazy.

"So calm down."

The argument kryptonite. No 'calm down' in the history of calming people down has ever calmed anyone down.

"I don't feel calm! I don't feel okay. That's the point!"

His face twisted, trying to understand what trip she was on.

"So what do you want?" he sounded irritated now.

"I don't know!" she was affronted by his tone. She was trying to think things aloud with him, like she should be able to with her partner. He was her *partner*. He wasn't being one right now.

"Nanki, isn't there too much upheaval already?"

Honestly, he just sounded tired. Nanki couldn't even blame him. This whole thing had been exhausting. From the outside it may look like a lack of movement meant an extended holiday of sorts, but the mental fatigue was real. Amidst everything else, there were still EMIs* to pay and salaries to be given, food and medical supplies to be bought, and enough savings to be able to afford treatment just in case. If they would be so lucky to even get it, that is.

It didn't help that the 'just in case' could be any bizarre amount of money. There really was no telling.

Nanki fell silent. He was right, what was she thinking?

* Equated Monthly Instalments

He sensed her energy deflate like a balloon within her. For a moment, she had dared to hope. For what, she wasn't quite sure. Just for something…bigger.

His voice softened. "Nanki, there is too much happening at the moment to be thinking clearly. Let's not uproot any more things right now, okay? Quite frankly, I have no bandwidth to deal with any more change. Do you?"

She stayed silent, not breaking eye contact.

He continued, "I mean, is this great? No, of course not. I wish I could not work either and just play cricket. I'm hanging on by the edge of my teeth to this job.

"For what? We are working on half our salaries, and you know if things don't change soon, we'd still have to dip into our savings within two months. Just to maintain the life we have now. What about next year? We are supposed to be having children at some point… How are we supposed to do this without holding on to whatever little stability we do have?"

Dammit. If he's going to go all rational on her… how would ridiculous dreams ever get fed? She frowned in annoyance.

This was check and mate and just like that she was trapped into the smallest square space of life.

The problem with asserting equality was the acceptance that it went both ways.

Just like she couldn't imagine Dhruv leaving his job to rethink life, jeopardising her comfort and stability, it wasn't fair of her to leave all their combined financial burdens on him either.

'Hmm…,' she nodded, resignedly.

He gave her a weak smile.

This is what it was going to be. This is *all* her life was going to be.

Here's the thing though: when you start understanding the gravity of death, you *learn* to weigh life—the thought gurgled up—demanding to be heard.

When it was so damn hard to stay alive, shouldn't living amount for *more*, somehow? Otherwise, what was the point of putting up such a fight?

These thoughts sprung up from somewhere deep inside her core, but froze into a lump in her throat, as she turned away stifling the tears welling up in her eyes.

***

'The mountains make a poet out of everyone.'

Later that evening, as she rested her back against the bed headboard idly, Nanki found herself in the middle of a conversation with herself, about nothing in particular.

As she grew conscious of it, she tried to listen in.

WHAT, woman?

WHAT do you need to say?

Well, *something* had to be said. If restlessness had a language, it seemed to have proclaimed.

Taking a cue from River, she felt the bizarre need to find the poetry within her too, so as to lend her emotions some much needed words.

Maybe then, they would stand a chance to exist.

She scrolled up till she found the first image River had ever sent her. The stoic mountain ranges bejewelling Rishikesh late at night.

Unchanging and majestic.

She remembered the tranquillity she felt that night and borrowed from it today. It was harder to come by now.

What was it about something that had existed since far before us—and will continue to, long after us—that makes it such a source of calm, she wondered. Maybe it's the standing testimony that some things are capable of weathering far more than we would ever have to. The mountain ranges, quietly witnessing an eternity and us, a mere ephemeral moment in the landscape of time.

And yet they survive…

So maybe, just maybe, you stand a chance too.

All the struggle in the world to become bigger and yet ironically, comfort was only found in feeling terribly small.

Then, she started to write…

What an odd moment in time,
To be feeling
The weight
and the weightlessness,
The meaning,
And the meaninglessness,
The purpose,
And the purposelessness
of the Artist
- and his Art,
Of Strife
- and its striving
Of Life
- and its living.

It felt important somehow to document this point in her life to remember where it got her. There was nothing remarkable about it, really, but it needed to be flagged.

Nanki left it on River's DM, as casually as leaving a note in her personal diary. She'd reflect upon it later.

This window *was* like her personal diary where she wondered all her random wonderments, but even better, because it responded back. Who knew River would end up becoming her personal human diary when she responded to that Bungy advertisement an eon ago.

To talk is great, but to b*e unconditionally heard i*s infinitely better, she thought as she gave a dry smile and left the chat to proceed with the rest of her day.

***

Is everything okay on your end?

River had hearted the poem, and asked in response. It was a couple of hours later and her phone had vibrated loudly in announcement.

Nanki realised she had never brought him into her everyday so far and she observed how odd it was to feel like you almost know someone without knowing a thing about them.

It was time to change that.

It's my grandfather. He is Covid-positive.

Silence.

Then, a minute later:

I am sorry to hear that.

Are you tiding through?

Now *that* felt like a real question she could answer. An empty show of solidarity only avoids having to dig deep enough to engage with the awkwardness of unstable emotions. She remembered having placated Kavya with empty words, and it had NOT been okay. She was grateful to have her struggle acknowledged. No one knew if it was going to be okay. Absolutely no one did.

River did the only genuine thing there was to do: Ask her if she was making it through.

Am I?

Hmmm, let's see…

Actually. I am not.

I am struggling.

I'm struggling tremendously.

With fear, with uncertainty, with making sense of any of this.

With understanding what it means to be alive in a dying world,

—with the guilt of it,

The unshakeable, unbearable guilt.

Of not doing better with that privilege.

Of such a living not amount to anything.

A living that is as good as not.

She typed the words furiously, mad at the world for throwing such a tantrum.

Yep, that is about it, she said rereading her message.

Sounds like this is about more than just Covid.

That aside, are you not happy?

Am I happy?

Ha! That question was almost….*cute*.

Aside from Covid, aside from lockdowns, who had she been and had she been happy?

Was she really and truly happy in her life?

Only psychopaths must be happy *all* the time!

Hahahah well, there's a difference.

No one can be happy all the time, it is true.

It is nothing to aspire for because it can never be real.

The human condition is far more complex than that.

We have to experience a myriad of emotions.

I say have to because we do. No one is exempt from it.

We have to feel everything there is to feel.

That is the nature of being alive.

But then we have to strive to create contentment amidst that chaos.

That is the nature of being human.

So, a more valid question to ask would be: Are you unhappy then?

Because if it is so, you will have to listen to your unhappiness.

Restlessness will persist for as long as you don't.

That is the nature of restlessness, no?

Nanki thought about that. She took a minute to think about it, in fact. Then five.

I guess I must be.

Happy, I mean.

In the sense that I am not sad.

And yet ...

She wondered if she should go on and decided upon it.

Something is missing.

Something has been missing for a while.

Ever so often, with a sigh, she would wonder:

What makes joy so tedious in a perfectly good life?

It's just that...

There is a little seed of void that sprouts up out of nowhere on some of the most ordinary days.

I don't know how to explain it...

After careful consideration, typing and erasing, and then typing some more, she finally wrote:

It feels like a moist spot on freshly dried sheets.

She sat back and read the response again.

This... This was it. She wondered where that feeling had come from.

I once tried placing its physical location in my body.
When I pictured it inside of me,
it looked like a little black hole in the centre of my chest
that sucked the joy out of my heart and limbs
and spat it into the infinity of the universe,
where it would be lost forever.
Do you know what's weird?
In those moments, I almost wished that something really was wrong,
so I could have an explanation.
Then of course, I would catch myself being an ungrateful brat,
say a prayer of gratitude and brush it off.
The humdrum of the day would drown the thought out
and lull me into an otherwise thankfully unthinking living outside of my head
and the moment would pass just like it came.
I guess,
it's easy to forget the noise of your thoughts when you're too busy going through the paces of a well-planned life,
designed to be the best version of the average.

The great Indian dream.

...

Then Covid-19 had hit the world.

Lucky me, now I found several hundred reasons to blame for that black hole.

What a yay, right?

Nowhere to hide from them anymore and no exit left open.

I had to sit with it, didn't I?

The more I thought about it, the more aggressively it grew,

As if the more attention I gave it, the more I kept feeding it.

It wasn't just a little black hole anymore, it became the big, growing darkness threatening to consume me, that I was simply existing inside of.

Somedays I think that it is now feeding on me instead.

The bigger it becomes, the smaller I become,

Till the blackness is everywhere and the light is just a speck.

He took a while to respond to this one, and Nanki re-read her own message a couple of times over till he did.

Nanki, I have a question. Where are you?

Where inside your body do you think you are?

Are you your skin, your eyes, your heart?

Nanki looked down at herself. She looked at her hands and turned her palms up. *Nope.*

She looked at her legs, and twitched her toes. Nope. That stubby toe isn't ME. Pretty as it was with the glittery nail polish: the things one does when they aren't bound by the protocols of playing an adult.

She touched her palm to her chest, trying to feel her heartbeat. It was hers and yet she didn't know how her heart felt to the touch or about the life it was leading inside of her. She wondered if it felt cared for, even though she had never really looked after it, not consciously anyway.

I mean I don't smoke…does that count?

Oh, wait, wasn't that for the lungs?

I'm sure the heart benefits from it too though.

She stood in front of the mirror and leaned in closer to look at her eyes. They seemed to give away a lot. She blinked deliberately, her eyes continuing to stare at themselves.

Was she her eyes? They seemed to be more like the *narrator*. Not the story. Nope.

Her body, her organs, the blood running through them, all felt like the caretakers outside of her— protecting her, *holding* her.

They were all an intrinsic *part* of her being but not the being itself.

Then where am I?

What are they taking care *of?*

She could feel her breath move up and down inside her. Her aliveness seemed to be intertwined with it.

Am I my breath?

She sputtered the words out loud even as she wrote them, exasperated.

What is a breath? You take in air that already exists outside, consume it till it fills you up, and you release it in the next second, making place for another.

Essentially, you draw from an infinity, let it flow through you briefly, leaving you and itself changed by its mere passage through you.

Isn't that so cool?

You consume a bit of infinity and it consumes a bit of you

and then, you release it back unto itself, although with a bit of yourself

—until one day you finally become one with it entirely.

Errrrm.

Are you saying I don't exist at all?

Seriously man. This is messing with my head!

...

How have you spooked me out of my self?

Physically speaking, where the hell AM I?

On the contrary, ma chérie,

You exist *infinitely.*

You are not your body.

You are nowhere in your body, and you are everywhere, all at once.

The question is WHAT am I?

The concept of 'I', is beyond the body.

The body is just our vessel.

Nanki thought about Nanu and his breath. She wondered if the infinity was planning on reclaiming his piece of itself, leaving his body behind. She dared to ask, knowing fully well that no answer imaginable could change how she felt about this:

Then why do we fear death so much?

We have always been afraid of what is bigger than us, haven't we?

Infinity always scares us. Terrifies us, in fact.

One always loves the waves but forever fears the ocean.

What is frightening is the inherent knowledge that you do not and cannot contain it,

but rather, that you are contained *by* it.

I've always found that rather arrogant

—to not embrace it just because we do not understand it.

And yet humans do it all the time. In life, as well as on the subject of death.

We *can* meet them both with equal equanimity.

What a hippie, thought Nanki. Sometimes she wondered if he was smoking some magic mushrooms or something. He very well could be. Who knows? She wouldn't mind getting in on that action. Only sometimes though, when she really needed answers.

Nutella, on the other hand, worked just fine for when the questions got too much.

Nanki sent an emoticon shaking her head.

Equity, I understand.

Equanimity, whaaa?

River went on,

It is the mastery of the mind to stay calm amidst chaos.

Not in a submissive way, but rather in a very carefully controlled manner.

It is the assured knowing that the reins are always—as they have always been—

in your hands.

When you enter a room, how do you sense the tension before you've heard a single word?

When you hear of betrayal, how do you instantly have that sense of dawning, like you knew this was coming, even before your mind has accepted it?

When you hear of someone you love dying, despite frantically going into denial, there is a part inside of you that goes cold, that just knows this has happened.

On the flip side, before a winning pitch, how do you know you've got this?

How do you feel the love of those that are far?

There is a place within you, of inherent knowledge, that is wise beyond your years and senses—what we like to call our gut feel.

Took me a while, but I know to trust it now.

My profession helped—it made me hypersensitive to the rise and fall of my energy and emotions.

When they oscillate in intense extremes, you realize very quickly that only the one who is not troubled by the waves can ride the tide.

I guess that's why assertive peace became a natural coping mechanism and a subject of intrigue for me.

Something I've since spent a long time studying.

That's why he was so good at this, Nanki thought. It came naturally to him—*assertive peace*, as he put it.

How do I get this in the here and now?

That would be for you to figure out.

All I know is, there is strength in knowing that the soul is eternal.

Haven't you heard

We were born from the stars, at the beginning of time?

We carry them within us

And so never has there been a time where your spirit has not existed,

nor will there ever be one where you cease to be.

What isn't, will never be. What is, will never cease to be.

And so, where is there any need for fear?

What is there left to do but just be alive?

Fully, wholly, really.

Fully, wholly...*really,* she repeated to herself.

She had goosebumps crawl up her skin. It was electrifying, this thought, but it was also pacifying. How extremely odd.

River went on, freeing her from the need to respond.

He was *teaching* her— no, it was less patronizing than that. He was sharing *his* experience of living with her and allowing her to make it her own. The oldest iCloud in the world: Empathy. Put your feelings out there and it exists for as long as its memory does, to be drawn from, to be inspired by, to build upon. If only, one cares to open the album.

You know what I see when I see people combat their fears?

That this duel with the dark exists in every moment.

Some moments we just sleep through it, others force us to wake up to it.

Some moments, it sneaks in taking over our consciousness and drowning us under,

In others, it honourably stands in front of us, forcing us to fight.

Like a moment at the edge—and isn't that so much better?

This duel between the light and the dark will always continue till one consumes the other, just like the day consumes the night, and the night plunders the day, going round in circles in an unending loop.

Oh, but when there is light...

Oh yes, indeed, Nanki thought, walking into her balcony to see the streetlamps coming on. It was too late for tea and too early for dinner. Nothing to do but watch those lights flicker. Not the worst bargain.

Why is it then,

that the first thing that the dawn of light does is cast shadows, pulling along a piece of darkness?

As if teasing it out to challenge itself?

That is a good question.

I'd imagine the answer to lie in the creation of existence:

You have been given a birth, and no matter how you live it, it is going to culminate in its death.

You have been given a functioning body, but it must always be in need of fuel through water and food.

You have been given a mind, that will always have to cope with restlessness

You have been given energy, but you will have to overcome inertia.

You have been given wisdom, but you must spend a lifetime unlearning first.

You have been given a whole life, but you have to make it through every day.

Now wasn't *that* true.

Exactly. Look at the patterns.

Sounds like God is a masochist, and we are the sufferers.

What an inefficient system we are.

Perpetually in need to just basically survive.

How awful is that!

Oh, but don't you see?

How beautiful that is....

We weren't just given an existence; we were also given its purpose.

Pretty neat in fact, isn't it?

We are alive, we have desires, we therefore strive, and in that striving, we create our living.

She paced within the little space and considered that. *Nope*, that did not sound right, wisdom-wise.

Not that it wasn't real. It definitely sounded relatable, but wasn't evolution supposed to be about going beyond the pettiness of this animalistic 'real' living?

Aren't we supposed to move towards giving up all worldly desires though?

Isn't that the ultimate benchmark of growth?

To find the peace in forsaking desires and material gains and earthly attachments?

Detachment and moksha and all that jazz.

You're confusing inherent desires with impulses.

One of the lamps refused to come on and stayed unlit. She felt a sudden hatred for it.

How can you tell the difference?

By how it feels, of course.

Our feelings are our greatest internal compass—our one guiding light.

If we can figure out how to tune into it, it will lead us to the shore.

Impulses will feel like passionless play. Scattered pursuits, the more of which you have, the more of it you will need.

Inherent desires are different: those will feel like prayer.

The deeper you dive into them, the lesser you will be wanting for.

It feels like the truth emerging and taking you along into its glorious wave.

The more you pursue it, the fuller you will get.

...Aah, now I get why it must be called *ful*filment.

Nanki traced the word in her mind with him and observed how much more beauty can be seen when standing on the outside.

Yes, it must, mustn't it.

Thanks River, I should get back now.

Oh by the way, how is your English so good?

Thank you for thinking that!

I had to be able to communicate with my jumpers when they're scared for their life!

Learning their language is the only way I can show up. I also know a little Hindi, but it's limited to the cook at my local Dhaba, when I need to tell him the food is 'bohot acha hai'.

Nanki grinned imagining his accented Hindi, then looked into the living room and sighed; dinner wouldn't cook itself.

Bohot acha hai.

She left the chat, inspired. She'd make Dhaba aloo today.

***

It was another evening and Nanki was brushing her hair, looking into the mirror. She straightened herself and looked closely at the reflection.

Her.

Not her.

It really was mind-bending every time she did this. River's chat had kept coming back to her and there was one part she wasn't sure of yet. She scrolled back.

So, the difference between inherent desires and impulses is the same as that between oats and Nutella, right?

Oat desires, then.

He was online but didn't respond for another fifteen minutes. She wondered if there were others like her that he was attending to. Putting out fires everywhere, this River, she thought.

If you say so!

laughing emoji

That's to be the whole diet, then? Oat desires?

You can drizzle the Nutella but it's not going to fill you up, is it?

Then what do you do to be full AND be satiated?

Those two things are *not* the same thing.

Have you ever tried making oats well? *tongue out emoji*

Hmph

Okay, but seriously, it's only worth it when you're consumed with it. 100 or nothing.

To build something solid out of your desire demands a one pointedness. Not an unfettered meandering, but rather consistently choosing to walk in the light of your own truth, till all else is blinded out. That's when you see it emerge.

And yes, that pursuit takes all the courage in the world.

Courage. The one thing she could feel depleting out of her, day after day.

River must've guessed her thought in her silence because after a moment, he wrote:

You think courage is about fighting what is standing opposite you, when courage is in fact what you have to fight inside of you. Always.

Protecting the ideal by acceptance of the battle is far greater than sitting back in renunciation.

The world doesn't stop burning just because you close your eyes.

Renunciation is born from great sorrow.

By definition, it is separating oneself from the experience of living.

Sometimes in exaggerated cases, even physically, but not always.

More often, people give up mentally and then call it wisdom.

To get so jaded that you don't allow life to draw you in is always a defeat, never a victory.

It is a pulling of oneself away, tearing something apart, taking great pain to hack away at the glue that holds you together.

Renunciation, as peaceful as it sounds, is intrinsically built of grave conflict, and has anything beautiful ever come out of conflict?

Is there really strength in detachment?

At this edge in your life, you say you are at, if you were in fact, standing at the literal edge, looking out at the vastness that is yours to conquer,

in Bungy, is there strength in letting go of the desire to jump, or is there glory in letting go of your internal fears?

Perspective is a gift, that you find lying behind you when you take that one step ahead.

So much of wisdom is shedding the delusions of intelligence.

It is the calm that transcends grief and anxiety.

Those exist *within* it, where it tears.

Peace isn't something that resides outside of you, that warrants you overcoming yourself in its pursuit: It is something that comes when you align *with* yourself.

As an integral piece of art in the design of the universe.

That black spot—sounds like it may be a tear in the being, the part where you get separated from yourself. A sign of disconnect. Get to it it so you can stitch it up. *smiley emoji*

Nanki sank into her chair. A *disconnect* from the self, a tear in the fabric of her being, she reverberated.

Are you suggesting I'm depressed?

I can't possibly know that.

I had read somewhere that one of the first evident signs of depression is when someone gives up on dressing up.

That is not to say that all well-dressed people are happy, nor that the ones living out of their PJs are depressed.

But one's outward appearance starts to reflect their inner ecosystem sooner than later.

It's like they've given up the desire to embrace the day, to look presentable, to show up.

Similarly, the clutter in your room is going to reflect a scattered mind.

When you're unwell, you lose your *will* to eat.

Appetite is a sign of *health*.

Whether it is your hunger for food or for dreams.

Attaching shame to it, then, is grossly misguided.

Nanki thought about how it was so much harder sometimes to know what your dreams even are.

It was easier to identify the nightmares. Maybe that's where one begins onwards that quest—knowing what you *don't* want. However one came upon that realization may even be irrelevant.

What if the chase of dreams disrupts the reality you have so carefully built though?

...

The problem with the jump is that it takes you away from the safĕty of the ground.

How is that not sacrilege?

She could hear Dhruv outside. There was some commotion in the hallway. She left her phone aside and got up to see. Dhruv was glued to the door to Nanu's room, singing rather badly, through the door to one of Nanu's favourite songs. Nanu, in turn, cranked up the volume and started singing too. She could hear his raspy voice in heartwarming pieces. Out of nowhere and all of a sudden, the music had pushed its way in.

It sat oddly, wedging itself in the middle of the now permanent, although intangible residents of the house: Emptiness and Fear. This cacophony filled their home, becoming its own entity, and took up real space, growing louder and bigger. So much so that the other two seemed to have been outweighed, forced to shrivel up, even if only briefly.

Leaning against the door frame, soaking the view in, she asked herself again: Was she happy? She looked over at Dhruv, seeing the man she had married peek outside his skin after a long, long time.

She loved how loving Dhruv was to her family. Always had. She loved him for how much Nanu loved him. She loved him for how the house lit up with their togetherness. She loved how they managed to stitch together their own little world amidst the Kishore Kumar music floating in from Nanu's Caravan, her narrating the day to the last detail, and Dhruv's laughter filling up the room—and for how in that home there was love.

That must be the same as being in love. And it must mean that there was happiness. It seemed to have been enough. Well, some days anyway. On days like this. And days like this carried her through the others…

She ran to her phone to capture it on video. Adding it to her Instagram stories, she wrote #CrazyStupidLove.

Before she knew it, the song had carried her into its music and she had joined in, breaking into a dance till as long as the song lasted. Then, the day returned to normal, but it mercifully left them with a bounce to their steps and a lightness in their hearts. That's how they knew that although the song had ended, the music lived on….

By the time she returned, her Instagram had a couple of unread DMs:

Sacrilege. *noun*.

A violation or misuse of what is regarded as sacred.

Had to look it up.

What a pretty word for something so devastating.

But I guess most devastating things *are* seen as terribly beautiful, aren't they?

We are so good at attaching such beauty to tragedy, and so much virtue to suffering.

Just as Nanki was getting lost in the poetry of his thought, he added,

Pardon my language, but THAT is utter bullshit.

Nanki snorted.

Hahahhahahahahah, I did NOT see that coming.

It is true! The world needs to stop with it already.

Romanticizing the idea of hurt and pain as a concept needs to be retired,

like YESTERDAY.

Your dreams and desires, your interpretation of the world and how you react to it,

how life happens to you and how you happen to it,

are all your unique footprint on this moment in time.

Denying any of it, for a false sense of virtue, for following someone else's idea of the ideal life,

now THAT is sacrilege.

It can only ever cause resentment, and you can't be of any use to anyone when all you are is a ball of resentment.

It comes to get us someday or another:

The truth that flows within you.

What a waste it would be for anyone to spend their lives diminishing themselves,

becoming smaller and smaller till nothing exists anymore,

just to fit into boxes that were always too small to contain them in the first place,

instead of honing those beautiful rough edges that stick out

and force the box to expand instead?

She looked over at Dhruv. He sat across from her, humming the tune to the song they had danced to earlier and she felt a rush of affection.

The lyrics invited her into them on their own, now playing inside her head.

Haal kaisa hai janaab ka…

Dhruv, her anchor in a crazy world, keeping her afloat, keeping her sane by standing next to her, rock-solid—being the one constant in an increasingly, maddeningly unstable world. She could never, ever hurt him. Annoying as he was sometimes.

That would be *sacrilege.*

Kya khayaal hai aap ka…

He looked up and seeing Nanki looking at him, started singing aloud now.

Hum tum to machal gaye ho ho ho…

His left shoulder joined the party in his head, doing a little dance.

Yun hi fisal gaye haa haa haaaa…'

She just sat there looking at him. This was the problem and herein lay her conflict. She realized she was a woman very much in love and in agony and in grief, all at once—with this man, with this world, with this life.

Sometimes the stakes are too high.

Sometimes you just can't.

It is a struggle that has existed since the beginning of time:

One trying so desperately to catch the voices of others in the room often turns deaf to their own.

The inability to detangle the threads, the black from the white, always plunged the world into an infinite grey.

There is a time for everything.

You won't, till you can't. But after that…

Eventually, we all become our own person.

When that happens, I hope you travel lighter,

and don't carry any guilt of what you leave behind, or of the stakes it cost you.

And I hope that then, you remember...

That a bird's song is just as sweet even when no one hears it.

What a shame it would be if the bird wouldn't sing in the absence of an audience.

The world would lose out on the song, and far more grievously, the bird on its singing.

For the sake of its beauty, I hope we let there be song *flying bird emoji*

Someday, she wished, she did in fact gather the courage to sing out her song but today, and right now, it was time to come back home.

6

It was a weird thing. Of course it had been a coincidence for her to rebrand the drink on the same day that Nanu had tested positive for Covid. Of course it was. But somehow it had gotten linked in her brain, as if one was the function of the other.

For the past ten days, she had stayed away from work, after having sent a cursory mail to Jaya informing her of the crisis on the home front and of her unavailability until further notice. She wrote of Nanu having tested positive, of them having to get tested, of their house being flagged as a containment zone. After that, she switched off, without waiting for a response, not having the energy to open emails, check her messages or take calls.

Whatever short-lived mojo she had got back, it seemed to have evaporated out of her like smoke, as quickly as it came. She would never admit it, but she secretly hoped that Nanu would get better by putting a solid distance between herself and this project. Even if it was just a crazy idea in her mind, she would not take a chance. If nothing else, what if these ideas become self-fulfilling prophecies? Like if you believe something hard enough, it becomes your truth?

Like *God*, she thought wryly.

It's something that she had been wondering a lot about recently. With all this time she now had, with nowhere to go, with nothing in her control, she wondered about the existence of a God.

She had never thought of herself as an atheist, nor did she associate with any kind of faith. Nanu was a religious man, and she always saw her mum bow her head to his God in front of him when she was here. She always suspected it was more out of love for her father than for God, but she followed suit anyway, without questioning it.

They never discussed religion at home, but Nanu would often read from his religious texts and narrate the most elaborate stories from what he referred to as sacred ancient history. It seemed no different than the other pretty fairy tales she had grown up listening to, although with far more characters than she could keep track of.

In the current dire situation, however, she needed to find an object to attach her faith to. Something that could give her strength. It would make life so much easier to just *believe* that help was on its way. Maybe it was, maybe it wasn't. But her faith would get her through. Maybe that was help enough. Maybe that was what faith was about.

Since it was just an esoteric concept, it couldn't be proven. But it also couldn't be *disproven*. The more intangible, the better, because how do you destroy something that exists as a belief inside your head?

What a sneaky little caveat, marketing-wise. This concept emerges from the depths of your fears, takes the form of your highest imagination of courage, and in doing so, gives you it. All coming from within you, all already existing within your energy field. You create the demand, you provide the supply, your faith guarantees the transaction. That's check and mate. Truly, the greatest brand of all. *God.*

A self-fulfilling prophecy.

Maybe if she would believe in her faith and a divine power as hard as she believed in her fears, that would become true too, and by believing it to be so, she could intensify the protection around them. This made practical sense. However, the fact of the matter was, that she didn't know where to start or how to really pray to please this almighty power to harness it.

Hmph, anyhoo.

Her current weird superstition seemed to be working, because it was almost ten days and Nanu seemed to be getting better. She would not so much as *open* her laptop till they could open his door.

The doctor had said that by the eleventh day, regardless of his symptoms and condition, he would no more be contagious, and he could resume accessing the rest of the house.

She was counting down the hours now. In some corner of the house, so was Dhruv.

***

It was nearing midnight. The tenth day was coming to a close. She was standing in her kitchen, impatiently brewing three cups of tea in anticipation, finally to be enjoyed together, huddled around him on his creaky old bed, in the same space, breathing in the same air.

She added all the spices he liked in his teas; although usually used individually, today she threw them in together: Cardamom, grated ginger, and some precious golden-orange strands of saffron. It was just about starting to smell like a festival in there, even as her phone beeped:

She read the time on her screen:

00:00

She swiped open her lock screen and jumped into her Whatsapp:

It was Nanu: "I free! If awake. Hug me."

He always had trouble locating the apostrophe on the keypad.

The screen blurred in front of her as all the tension of everything seemed to wash away all at once. It was finally over.

All the tears she had never cried sprung up now as she ran to his room, clutching her phone hard.

He was sitting up in his bed against the headboard, freshly bathed and all dressed in his off-white kurta, the last few strands of his grey hair combed neatly back, arms open to welcome his little girl into an embrace. It was as if he had been carefully, painstakingly even, getting ready for a celebration.

It *was* one. In that little room on a random midnight, huddled together in the heartiest of hugs, it was quite simply the greatest celebration there ever was. She cried, he cried and at some point Dhruv had joined the hug and amidst a flurry of kisses and tears, there was the smell of an all-spiced tea that filled the room.

Dhruv had brought in a tray of her tea in their finest china and kept it on the mantle.

She didn't know it then, but she would remember that fragrance for the rest of her life as the smell of a miracle.

***

Over the next few hours, she allowed the relief to wash over her. She in fact, let herself get drenched in it. It was almost morning now, but the sun showed no signs of letting the world know.

Nanki wanted to scream from the rooftops and let everyone know that all was well in 26, Kalyan Enclave. She wanted to tell the neighbours and the strangers, and she *really* wanted to tell Jaya—more in the capacity of her mentee, than her employee. She didn't want to discuss work still. However, she felt the kind of joy right now that makes one feel...*invincible.*

If I have this, I can face the rest of the world, she thought, looking fondly at Nanu snore next to her.

They had both slept the night in here, with Dhruv having dragged out their musty spare mattress from their storage under their bed. It was placed perpendicular to Nanu's bed, although on the floor, and he now lay on it, fast asleep.

They had stayed up for another hour just talking. Of health and sickness, of fear, of courage. Also of food, of chai and of neighbours. It was everything and nothing, really.

As she sat there now, ruminating over it, she realised what a privilege it was to feel the joy in the nothingness of their every day.

Funny, how that was everything, Nanki thought now. It's the nothingness that takes up most of the time anyway. The time in-between the everything. When there's a peace of mind within that, it buoys up the rest, like a steady sea holding up the ship. However, when there's chaos raging within the nothingness, there's not a thing to be done to keep one from drowning.

Now that she was here, in that place of peace, she picked her phone up to call Jaya. It was 06.04 am.

Too early, she thought and decided to leave her a text instead.

"Morning Jaya! We're Covid free! With Nanu now. He's doing okay. Just wanted to let you know. Thanks and hope you're well." Sent.

She had dozed off again, when an hour later her phone vibrated 'off the hook', if mobile phones could have a hook to fall off of.

"H-Hello?" she croaked, her eyes still shut.

"Hallelujah, she's alive!" It was Jaya, her cheery self in all its glory, way too before coffee. Regardless, it was nice to hear her voice after what felt like an eternity.

"Good morning Jaya!" She faked the energy while sitting up straight in involuntary respect.

"Wake up, sleepyhead! How's Nanu keping?"

"So far, so good. Still has cough and shortness of breath, but we can be with him now, so that's a big thing."

"I'm so glad to hear it. He's a fighter...you take after him, you know."

Nanki rubbed her eyes. She didn't know where that came from or even if it were true, but she sure wished it was.

"Hmm...you're missed around here, kiddo. I assume you haven't been checking your mails. Your idea got through!"

Oh no, no, *noooo......*

"Err...." she started to protest to stop her right there, but Jaya continued full steam.

"The beverage Nanki! They are changing the composition of the drink..." Her heart dropped to the floor.

"...we've had consecutive con-calls with the team, all heads of departments and they are so excited with this rebrand, AND...." Nanki could hear the exclamations in her sentences. She instinctively looked towards Nanu. He was still asleep.

"...they want you to lead this account! We've got the approvals, the plan is taking shape and we are raring to go! At this rate we should be ready for launch by the next quarter..." Silence.

There, she said it. It was over.

"You understand what that means? I was forty by the time I led my first full-fledged campaign. You've done it! You've skipped the steps and climbed the ranks, my brilliant, brilliant child!"

Nanki sat there, blowing air into her cheeks, dumbstruck.

"T-that's so great."

She could sense Jaya be confused on the other end of the line. Regardless, she didn't probe further and politely ended the conversation soon after.

Nanki continued to keep her fingers tightly crossed—reverting to her high school instinctive gesture to ward off any oncoming bad luck.

7

What is success?

As a lull hung upon the cold afternoon several hours and cups of tea later, Nanki contemplated over the race that she was in—and apparently winning. She hadn't told anyone yet. Saying it would make it real, and she wasn't quite ready for that. For now, it could be on pause. A maybe or a maybe not.

River seemed to never have anything better to do than indulge her existential crisis.

It is different things to different people.

But mostly, it's having gone a step further today than where you were yesterday.

It is the movement of growing.

Why do we chase it?

We don't ask a rose why it lives to bloom...

When we grow,

it means we have moved forward

and in doing so,

moved closer to reaching our highest potential—

one that only we knew the existence of

and therefore are responsible to deliver to the world.

It means there was potential,

there has been momentum,

and there is now succession.

It validates the inner workings of our mind to our own selves.

Stagnation is not natural to any living being.

It is a characteristic trait of only non-living things.

Only a stone sits unmoving.

Ageing is itself motion and motion is a sign of life.

Stagnation breeds sickness,

rotting life and health away.

When people get comfortable in their stagnation,

there will always be a rotting of emotional and mental health.

So most simply, to succeed is to evolve.

And we chase it because

we can't stand to stay stagnant.

Life calls to us to move.

What does that have to do with money?

Nothing at all. Why do you ask?

She gave out a chuckle. He was most unassuming, this man.

In case you didn't notice,

people equate your life's success

with professional success and money.

In case you didn't notice,

other people's opinions

aren't the greatest barometer to live your life by.

Making money is just one skill.

It's a great skill

but it's just one thing to be good at.

Like someone is great at painting,

someone is great at football,

someone is great at making money.

I'd rather be great at being happy.

When that happens,

I find I become better at making others happy too,

and that brings me joy.

They aren't necessarily exclusive,

but they aren't necessarily related either.

But maybe I'm just a people pleaser—

lucky for me, it also brings me 'success'.

...

The conventional connotation of success

could fit into a teeny tiny box.

When people grow bigger, they aspire to *grow bigger*.

To actually occupy more space under the sun.

With fame,

It's to occupy more space in the minds of other people.

With money,

It's to occupy more physical space on earth.

That in itself is quite a small thing to aspire for,

because growth is anything but finite.

Money can also mean a livelihood, freedom, and strength.

It can be wildly empowering, but

your chase can only last as long as your motivation does.

It is a means to an end, not the end itself.

Often though,

the motivation is just to be more.

Like you're 'less' as you are—

and that is a never ending, insatiable hunger.

The need to grow bigger for big's sake

must come from a desolate sense of smallness.

No amount of monetary success

can buy an inherent sense of prosperity though.

That comes from inside.

And if it's an inside job,

then you might as well fix that first.

What can be a bigger failure

than monetarily succeeding

yet finding lasting fulfilment elude you?

Then where do you go?

Success is whatever it means to you.

It's the intention that makes the difference.

When movement comes from a place of passion,

from a place of goodness,

it automatically invites success—

but that was not what it chased.

It happens *anyway*.

However, it is important for goodness to succeed.

When goodness succeeds, goodness thrives.

It comes from an internal ecosystem

of hope (not greed) and fulfilment,

and thereby, creates more of it.

Doesn't this constant need to be in motion
breed restlessness though?

In the absence of consciousness,
it very well does.
Experiencing unease is a precursory,
mandatory step towards change.
It presents the greatest opportunity to grow.
However,
it isn't about renouncing motion
and searching for peace in stagnation,
rather it is about learning to cultivate
a restfulness *within* motion.
Giving up outward action
but indulging it in the mind is only hypocrisy.
As long as it exists within your thoughts,
it exists—as real as the sky and the earth.
Refining one's thoughts—
That's where the work is required.
The actions will take care of themselves.
But that's tricky too: Not even all your thoughts are your own.
Only once your thoughts have been detangled
from others', from social conditioning, from delusions and ego,
do you come upon your own.
Raw, unprocessed, pure.
From there,

I allow the actions flow unabashedly—

a crystal clear reflection of the mind that thinks it,

without any worry of reward or its lack thereof.

She thought about her raw, unprocessed thought and how many times it called her to murder a Jeff and leave a Dhruv.

I don't think that'd work out so well for me...

She almost snorted.

Imagine the catastrophe

if people gave in to their unprocessed thoughts,

without a care for social repercussions.

You don't trust humanity much, do you?

tongue-out emoji

No comments.

Do you remember as a child, when someone tells you that unicorns exist, your only reaction is of amazement? Not skepticism.

You are accepting of the wonders of the world, even if you cannot see them.

We were never born to doubt the magic and the unknown of the universe,

but we for sure learn it.

Our natural state of being is that of peace and harmony and curiosity.

That's how we were born, and then we learnt conflict and resistance, and apathy.

You are born trusting everyone around you, then you learn fear and separation.

What we never had to learn was how to love—but we had to learn to hate.

What does that tell you about nature and nurture? The divinely ordained living vs the societally dictated one?

Our natural state is contentment, and we feel misaligned every time we move away from it.

So, it isn't at all about people reverting to animalistic tendencies in cutting out the external noise.

It is in fact about *returning* to human tendencies.

Which is how only hurt people *hurt* people.

Only resentful people feel the excessive need to confine others to their own limitations.

Only people who have lost their joy would cause pain to others.

Isn't that so interesting? That even at our worst, we fight to belong.

It is so painful to be misaligned with the world around us that if we cannot mirror the joy in it, it must mirror the pain in us. Then, we can fit. Then, we can feel sane and normal, because 'normal' is nothing but a poorly attributed function of how we align with our environments.

Therefore, we crave an equilibrium. Our hopeless way of feeling connected with our external environment is to have it look like our internal one. We *need* to feel one with it.

If the storm inside is stronger than the spring outside, it becomes intolerable.

Instead of becoming one with it, we try to make it one like us.

But energy is infectious. If you carry agitation and conflict within you, you can't help but spill it onto those around you and cause it to multiply. By suffocating the peace around you, you only continue subjecting yourself to even more suffocation, but at least now you're not the only one.

No one wins, but everyone loses equally. That's one kind of equilibrium.

The great news is that that can also be true of love and joy.

Shouldn't we change the algorithm then?

How does one stay within love and joy

when one is constantly being pulled in different directions?

Ah, now *that's* the game, isn't it?

People have different ways of doing that.

There's no one right way to do anything, of course.

But the end goal is to have a daily discipline

of staying centred and in your higher life condition

and by fiercely maintaining energetic hygiene.

Simply put,

purify the energy you dwell in and therefore give out,

AND be careful of what kinds of energies you welcome in.

Ooh! Energetic hygiene sounds so fancy... pray, do elaborate.

Yep, he was moving into hippie mode again. The inside of his mind was a fascinating place to visit. She imagined it was painted in eclectic neons.

Well, the French are known for fancy, so what can I say—it just comes naturally to me *winky face emoji*

It means becoming conscious to the energetic exchange that you are constantly engaged in.

You can never control how others think and act, but you can choose who and what you engage with.

Be very mindful of the energies you interact regularly with.

Observe what mental state it puts you in after that exposure.

Does an encounter raise your vibration and inspire you or does it drain you, or anger you?

Does it lift you up and make you feel lighter or does it feel like an emotional battering?

Whatever their energy, it will rub off on you.

How it makes you *feel* will stay with you long after they are gone.

Become aware of these experiences, and the people in them.

Their voices become the voices inside your head—

and before you know it, they become your own.

It could drive you crazy,

if you aren't vigilant.

Yes, it could...

Let's say one does manage to keep negativity at bay.

The absence of negativity isn't always positivity though.

It's a boring neutral sometimes.

How does one rise up from there into happiness?

By *choosing* to.

And being disciplined about that choice.

To not get pulled out of your contentment and sense of peace by situations, people and external forces demands a tremendous amount of discipline and conscious effort.

This is true for both, the presence of problematic triggers and the absence of exciting ones.

They are all just vehicles to take you home anyway—none of them are the destination.

It takes reconnecting with your 'self' energy daily.

Creating pockets of routine every day that strengthen and celebrate it.

For some that may be prayer, chanting, meditation...whatever else have you.

Your emotional gym, I guess.

Just like organizing the home button on your mobile phone: All other apps simply exist in it *winky face*

Nanki giggled away the weight of her dilemma and let the light-heartedness of the chat take over.

What do these saintly, consciously happy people look like, please?

She was partly amused while another part of her was genuinely curious now.

Hahaha, well historically,

We've always painted enlightened people as having a halo, haven't we?

Maybe in reality, it isn't an external light shining around them,

it is their internal light burning bright from within them.

Ironically, they are the ones who make life look most effortless.

Joyful, breezy and *worth* the journey. A privilege, even.

But as we all find out eventually, effortlessness takes the most effort of all.

They could fool you into thinking that they've just had it better,

when in reality, they've just *lived* it better—and it shows.

People who are successful at cultivating lasting happiness in their lives

act from a place of peaceful detachment because they do not need external joys.

They don't need it at all.

Their joy springs from within them and in abundance.

They can then carry it unadulterated, into their environments.

They continue to act, not out of cravings, impulses or desires,

but with a joyful responsibility

to deliver the liveliness of their life

for the aliveness of the world.

Time is a mental limitation.

An illusion.

A human way of bookending a scary infinity by breaking it down into small pockets that we can understand and engage with and exist within.

Its fascinating, isn't it? How the Universe though, is far too infinite to exist in time, but rather time exists within it.

Why put so much value on success and attach so much pain to failure, then?

When you aren't trying so hard to find a predetermined pattern, and actually *seeing*, as an observer, the nuances of the world and your life in it, you may arrive upon a far more authentic living.

That was all well and all, but…

What if one finds weaker minds preying on their energy and joy?

Energy vampires, she thought.

Office politics often brought them out in seemingly decent people. Men hated being contradicted by women and resorted to mansplaining all of life to them to assert their imaginary superiority. Superiors often devalued better opinions if they came from juniors and overrode them regularly. Everyone tried to be louder than the other and it was basically a ruthless energetic stampede. There was enough condescension going around to force a saint to kick back.

Meet them the same way you would an underprivileged person—with kindness.

They need it the most!

She had just started to sip some water, when this response made her choke on it.

Spluttering it out, she typed:

That's just great.

I'd be sweeping the floors within the week, River!

Gosh, you really aren't meant for the corporate world, you know? *tongue-out emoji*

Oh, I know.

Howeverrrr...

The trouble with the rat race is even if you win, you're still a rat.

The quote isn't mine, but the sentiments are.

Hahahhaha, so what

your solution is to leave all jobs and become a Bungy jumper?

Preferably. *laughing face emoji*

But where that's not possible,

to simply carry the spirit of the Bungy jumper into your corporate job would do just fine.

What a *relentless* salesman!

And what does that spirit look like?

One that knows

that life is in the moments.

It's the greatest learning from the edge:

that it's always going to be your relationship with yourself that counts in the end.

Stay above the negativity.

Don't cut down the life in your years by getting drawn into other people's inner drama when they try to suck you in.

If someone is out of alignment from their natural state of being

of love and peace and unconditional acceptance,

let them not take you with them, nor should you need to shake them out of it.

Just let the light within you burn stronger than the darkness within them.

The one that weighs more, wins and consumes the other.

Let not them pull you into their darkness, but you, with your grace and your unshakeable sense of self and harmony,

throw them the light to see a way out.

They will only see it when they are ready to see it.

Allow them their journey too.

It isn't your job to protect them from a path they have chosen for themselves.

Sure, she muttered under her breath. Jeff can have his journey to un-stupidify himself.

She looked up at Nanu who sat snuggled in the living room, swathed in his shawl, watching television. He had definitely diminished in the space he occupied. Looking at his frail frame now, she noticed how blissful he looked, regardless.

A freshly ironed kurta again today.

She knew this was his way of expressing gratitude for having made it. He was thanking the day for coming in and not having given up on him. He welcomed it with open arms the way he welcomed her into an embrace last night. He had always been a happy man, but he dressed up for these simple pleasures now like they were his biggest blessings.

Some days, success looks like having made it to the living room from the bedroom, and some days, that can amount to infinitely more than leading an international brand account in the most successful MNC* of the country.

How can you tell the difference?

Between if you're motivated by greed or by passion?

Oh *that* is the simplest thing in the world:

It is the difference between doing things for love

—and *from* love.

And somewhere within that journey, lies all of our morality and evolution.

It is as simple and as difficult as that.

...And that was everything she needed to know.

***

For love or *from* love.

That evening she gave herself the permission to entertain what she had been swatting away for lack of it making any perceivable sense. This time, it wasn't impulsive. With fierce mindfulness she googled the contact details of something that had taken refuge in her head since a random encounter in the wee hours of a December morning—

A little group of people called Dharma Foundation.

* (Multi-National Company)

8

NANU was definitely still grappling. It had been almost half a month since he had tested positive and four days since he had stepped out of isolation. As she sat in the living room, chopping *bhindi* for dinner, she watched him keenly.

There was a perpetual wheeze now, his breathing was tedious, his appetite wasn't the same and his body moved with a new tiredness.

While Nanki was deliberately focussing on counting the milestones and basking in the progress, there was no hiding from it: it was not yet behind them. At this point, it really felt like she was racing down an accident prone road, terrifyingly fast to just get out, decidedly not looking back or around at any collateral damage. Just as long as she made it to the other end.

Nanki felt weirdly responsible. There was a lingering guilt at having invited the work call in. To make up for it, she spent the days scouring the internet for all the hacks to beat what damage the virus had left behind. Almost obsessively so.

They sat in the sun by eleven am everyday sucking on a citrus fruit. Something to do with Vitamin C boosting immunity.

They switched over to drinking warm water from copper pots all day instead of their usual refrigerated plastic bottles of water. 'Delete the toxins out of your life' a popular wise man on TV had said. She wasn't sure of his credentials; all he did was *be wise.* So she let him be it.

They took an online Yoga meditation class every day. A calm, harmonious and happy mind was the best protection one could get, they said. For eight thousand rupees a month, she very much counted on it.

They added into their nightly routine what her grandmother used to call a Kadha. A traditional Ayurvedic recipe passed down from generation to generation in India as a shield against all cold and sore throat related symptoms. She had to ask her mother for the recipe. It was the most disgusting liquid she had ever ingested but the whole family seemed to swear by it, so she plodded on. It was a potion made by boiling down herbs and roots and spices, on a low flame for about an hour till it was reduced to a black syruppy goop. It tasted as bad as it looked, but every time she had it, she could feel the heat of it trickle down to every last cell, warming her from the inside.

Every time it did that, she looked up and said a mental *thank you* to her grandma for coming through for them, even long after she was gone. Nanki hadn't known her too long, so she didn't have a lot of memories with her.

Just a couple of passed down recipes and a ton of warmth.

Maybe that's what grandmothers were.

She didn't quite know if any of this was working in the slightest, but what else was there to do other than hope?

There was also another thing though.

The community Whatsapp group had been circulating a notice for a conference prayer meet this weekend. Dhruv as usual, wouldn't even have opened it.

It said that collective prayer had a higher healing frequency on account of the pooling in of energy. She wondered if God was getting old too. He must be going deaf if he needed to be yelled out to through a telepathic trumpet these days.

She would never admit it out loud but she considered joining in. If nothing else, it could be a crash course on how to do this prayer business.

***

By Saturday morning, Nanu was weaker still. He was getting thinner every day and his cheeks were sallow now.

Dhruv was asleep at six am, when Nanki slipped out of the bedroom to attend the prayer meeting being held on Zoom.

They had been given a mantra the day before that they had to chant together. It was a Sanskrit prayer, written in English. Consisting of four extremely long and extremely complicated lines, she had to learn them to chant along.

Their meaning was written in English below which translated to a praise of their deity, an acknowledgement of His power (Nanki winced at 'his'), and a calling in to protect them.

Extremely sceptical, she did it anyway. Nothing to lose, she told herself.

It went on for an hour with more participants than she had anticipated. It started with a man she didn't know, freshly bathed, extremely awake and unusually motivated, leading the meet. He introduced himself and said that he intended to make this an every weekend affair upon seeing the overwhelming response of the neighbourhood. Then, they just jumped right into it.

No protocol, no instructions—just a sitting in front of the laptop, chanting garbled words into the screen. Feeling like a monkey in a zoo, she just started aping their moves. How others sat, how they spoke, the intonation, the decibel.

They just chanted and chanted and chanted. Some with folded hands, some with eyes closed, some distracted but mumbling along anyway.

It was nice seeing the neighbours after so long. It felt nice to be part of the community, struggling together and striving together. It was comforting to be sitting in the balcony amidst her plants, consciously praying. The idea of it was nice anyway.

But faith? She wasn't sure if she felt *that*, but she tried really, really hard to copy that too.

***

Secretly, Nanki chanted for the next five days. Morning and evening.

Nanu was showing no tangible improvements and the doctor on call suspected his lungs had been affected. Nanu refused to get any more tests done saying he was getting by just fine.

He drank a lot more tea than usual and seemed to relish it even more slowly.

He asked for his favourite foods to be made every day even though he barely had an appetite.

He asked to be around wherever Nanki was in the house even though he didn't seem to have much energy to talk. He just sat back, wrapped in his shawl draped over his choicest kurta every day, looking out at the world just *blissfully.* She wondered what on earth he was so blissful about, but he made for a pretty sight.

He looked content and beautiful.

By the sixth day, his cough seemed to have taken on an aggressive turn.

Do you believe in God?

Nanki asked River that afternoon, honestly scared and desperate for miracles.

I do

What do you know about Him?

Him. She had no energy to fight this vestige of old sexism right now and gave in to tired submission.

That we will never fully know Him.

But we will always be known.

Sounded like the tagline of a creepy murder mystery. God... she tried to visualise the concept and failed. She looked out at the sky instead and asked,

If we ever find ourselves needing to get in touch,

how would we start?

By getting in touch with ourselves.

Our life force is the closest divine creation we get access to.

I will never know everything about the world there is to know.

Nor will I ever fully comprehend the infinity of God or the wisdom of the universe.

But I know a little about me.

I find that's enough.

My only real knowledge about the world is my awareness of myself.

So, every new day, I try a little harder, to know a little more.

That's what I call meditation, and that's my prayer. I close my eyes, and watch as my breath rises and falls, like the sun, the moon, the day, the night—the life.

I come to the consciousness of God moving through me, as life, and I simply observe his art in motion through my being.

I acknowledge, I appreciate and so, I harness.

In turning inward, in honoring myself, I let myself become an instrument for Godliness to flow through,

unobstructed even by me—

that is my way of devotion.

She fell silent.

What brings you to this question today?

My grandfather...

I just don't want to lose him.

Aah, ma chèrie.

You could never lose him.

We could never own people, even if we desperately wanted to.

So we don't even have them in the first place—nor do we even hold them briefly.

We just share time.

Heartbreaking and heart-healing, all at once: *We just share time.*

***

It always came back to this. Time was all there was.

As the evening rolled around, Nanki skipped her chanting session to sit beside Nanu as they sipped on hot masala chai with Parle-G glucose biscuits. It was tradition to dunk them into the tea, scramble to eat a bite before the rest caved in the moment it touched the hot liquid, and then follow it up by a generous gulp. By the end, the fallen remnants collected at the bottom of the cup and were dredged out with the glee only a puddle of sugary goodness can bring.

Despite the butter Danish cookies becoming a pantry staple now, this was still the epitome of comfort. Those just didn't crumble the same.

Nanu had been lying down on the sofa in the living room since morning. Not necessarily asleep, not awake either. The heater had been humming all day long, having stayed on to warm his shawl.

The frigid Delhi winter was as unrelenting as every year, Covid-no bar. His wheezing had been constant today and he had had to work much, much harder to draw in the icy cold air into his lungs.

Breath after breath after breath.

It was tiring just listening to him. It was heart breaking seeing him having to struggle. Nanki felt a sickening helplessness take hold of her.

There was not a thing she could do. She had never felt more *useless*.

Nanki had shut all the doors and windows to keep as much of the cold out as she could. Dhruv had brought out their old shawls and wrapped them around his feet to keep them warm.

It was only when she brewed some hot ginger tea that he sat up, eager and waiting. Although he was highly diabetic, she couldn't help adding the Parle-G he so dearly loved, to his tray today.

Always having been a coffee person, after all the lockdowns now, she had a new respect for tea. Nothing brought families together in India like chai.

As she sat looking over at him truly relish his steaming mug, she moved to sit closer to him, holding his free hand in hers. He smiled warmly, asked her no questions and clutched back tighter.

Despite his hands being wrinkled and weak, it still had the effect of making her feel shielded somehow, protecting her from the world. She was safe here.

She thought back to what River had said about communicating with God and she found herself close her eyes, and watch her breath rise and fall.

Slow down, she heard herself think.

From the fear, the emotions, the helplessness, the denial....

Letting go of what she was desperately trying to see—or fighting not to see, she instead inhaled deeply and braced herself to see what actually *was*.

She became aware of Nanu's hand in hers, warming even in their cold. She imagined her breath trickle down to her fingertips and into his, as if trying to reach within him and feel what he was feeling—if not to lessen his burden, maybe to share it with him, just for a heartbeat.

She didn't know if she imagined it, but she suddenly felt like she could.

Suddenly his breath was all she could hear in the room. She became aware of his presence and she could feel the force of his life—a piece of an infinite God—flowing through him.

Flowing *out* of him. Slowly, steadily, painfully, beautifully.

He knew.

Her eyes flew open. She could sense it now, quite inexplicably.

He knew, didn't he?

That was why the kurta, the favourite foods, the following her around.

He wasn't welcoming the day in… he was saying goodbye.

As her eyes brimmed with tears, she watched him as he sat bundled up inside his shawls, merrily reaching for another biscuit. It was the first time in the day where he looked remotely close to being comfortable.

She brought in her other hand and clasped it over his. Her palms grew closer in prayer, clutching his tightly in the middle. With no time left for further insecurity or research on how to reach God, she bowed her head and just asked for *help*.

As she turned inwards, the prayer came to her on its own.

Surprising herself, her deepest desire didn't ask for stretching out his pained living.

How had she been so selfish…

She found she couldn't bring herself to keep him around any longer than his health allowed him. Dragging out his days so she didn't have to face his absence—that was not for her to ask for.

All she wanted was for him to be well. To not have to suffer anymore.

'Thank you. Just thank you for our time. I will always be so, so grateful to have gotten to experience this. His love and his light. With all the love in my heart, please strengthen the protection around him. I pray for him to be in his highest life condition—whatever that is. I pray to attract whatever is absolutely the best for *him*.

Please just protect him. Please be there for him. Please be there *by* him.'

As far as prayers go, it was a fairly simple one, really.

No rituals, no right way of saying it, not even the right posture maybe. Yet in her gut Nanki knew this was the sincerest prayer she had ever mustered, maybe the sincerest one to have ever existed. Somehow, she knew without a doubt that it had reached its destination.

Years later she would recount this as her first real encounter with faith.

When she opened her eyes, Nanu was downing the last of his tea.

Quite anticlimactic, considering she felt like she had just taken an express tour of heaven and hell and back, while he sat here just the same, in their little living room, fishing out the last of his beloved beverage.

They spent the rest of that evening talking about things that mattered. Things that had been left unsaid, for no real reason.

She told him about her promotion and he exclaimed and clapped his hands, elated. He smoothed his palm over her head in blessing and told her he'd always be proud of her. That she will always be that girl who could achieve whatever she set her heart to.

"That *is* the problem. Mine just isn't in it anymore" Nanki whispered it, almost afraid that reality would hear her before she knew what to do with it.

"Beta, do anything in the world but never *ever* betray your heart. That's the only betrayal you will never get over...I would never want that life for you", he whispered through rasps.

She showed him where she was starting to see the first signs of ageing on her face and how it scared her. She tilted her face to highlight the new wrinkles that were beginning to form at the edges of her eyes now.

He cupped her face in his palm and said, "Lucky girl! Now you have proof of having smiled long and hard enough for your face to have moulded around its lines. Just like the fold lines that impress themselves permanently upon a fragile piece of paper—a map of where it has been."

She told him about River, and he said, "See, how important it is to surround yourself with good people?"

Yes, she thought, how beautiful that somedays goodness is simply sending a picture of a Himalaya mountain to a person on a lonely night in isolation far, far away from its beauty.

Nanu had a riminiscing quality even when talking about his present, "how odd a time to live through, where getting Rishikesh to a person stuck in Delhi can become just as meaningful as bringing water to a person stuck in a parched desert."

Most of all, they spoke about how Godliness can always be found in the unlikeliest of times and places.

They video called Ma and kept the call going for the entire evening. They enjoyed a virtual dinner together. They had managed a Kofta Curry with rice today. It took both her and Dhruv's efforts to get that ready. They turned up the volume on his Caravan as they sat to eat.

'Tera Mujhse hai pehele ka naata koi….'

Mum put down her spoon on the other end of the line, and started singing exuberantly for Nanu.

Dhruv and Nanki followed suit…

'Yunhi nahi dil lubhaata koi…..'

Nanu smiled his brightest smile and clapped his hands together to the chorus:

'Jaaney tuuuu, yaa jaaney naaaa'…

That night, they set the mattresses in his room again. They'd all huddle up and sleep together, they decided. She kissed Nanu on his forehead and told him she loved him. He hugged her and told her the same.

Holding his hand, they drifted off to sleep.

Nanu never woke up again.

Heart-breaking as it was, Nanki knew she had been given the greatest gift someone in this time could ask for: She got to say goodbye.

It was a privilege denied to too many people stuck in Covid wards, in isolation, in hospital waiting rooms. Families weren't even allowed access to the bodies after death, let alone to cremate them with due respect. People couldn't say goodbye to their children, their spouses, their parents as they died gasping for air, alone and suffering.

She would always remember that, on their behalf. She would always let that fuel her going forward, because now she *knew.* She *knew* their pain in knowing her privilege of getting to say her goodbyes, and letting Nanu know just how much she loved him. In holding his hand even as he slipped through her fingers.

We just share time.

She *got* to share hers—and what a beautiful evening they had made of it.

It had been a befitting farewell.

9

NANKI looked out the window at the busily humming street, tucked cosily within a pocket of Malviyya Nagar in Delhi and let the cool February air bathe her. It was a quarter past seven, the sun had set a while ago and she felt exhausted.

It had been thirteen days since the passing of her maternal grandfather, her Nanu as she called him—and the culturally appropriate quarantine for grieving was almost up. This marked the end of the official mourning period and she still felt completely out of her depth to even begin processing it.

"It is believed that the soul of the deceased hangs around for thirteen days be- be-be-cause it is unable to sever ties with its physical body," Mom had shakily explained on call, unabashedly breaking into hysterical crying, yet again.

She couldn't come from Ooty because travel was still prohibited, particularly for senior citizens. It was a terrible state of affairs, but no more terrible than what was now usual.

Oh, she had loved him so, so much—a love that Nanki had inherited in its entirety.

As per instruction, she patiently waited around the house she grew up in, for a sign of his astral presence and looked keenly—she hadn't much taste for traditions, but she didn't negate them entirely either. The right way to explain it would be that she didn't quite think about them at all.

But, she had thought, if ever there was a moment to believe....

Added to that was the pressure of arranging a virtual funeral, demanding her to strike a healthy balance between conveying gloomy somberness along with a package of the best pure ghee laddoos *from Haldiram only*, as mum had insisted.

This is how the thirteen days came and went. All the mystic action the house witnessed was how it neatly and surely shrunk him out of existence, as if he had been dead a long time.

His rocking chair was packed into the storage, his shawl that *always* lazily sprawled across the sofa, was folded into the cupboard and his favourite tea mug now laid idly at the back of the pantry. *Traitors.*

His Caravan music box lay mute and grieving, a solemn receptacle for the dust of the days.

This one hurt her the most. It's like he took the music of her home with him and now it lay cold and bare and hurting.

All of this was too much to contain within regular grief because you see, at thirty-three, this was the first and closest death she had ever witnessed. No matter what age that happens at, it leaves one small—wounded, abandoned and lost.

And that's where Nanki found herself that evening, as she stood staring out the window.

Her phone lit up.

River had shared a picture of hers from her own Instagram with a clap emoji.

Oh, she thought, this was a press clipping from two years ago.

AdWeekly Magazine had featured her as one of the young Brand Strategists of India to look out for in the coming years, 'Nanki Mehta, a vivacious 30-something professional in an envious job in advertising, married to her childhood sweetheart and an overall #bosslady'

As she looked at it now, it felt like it belonged to a different time.

Nanki Mehta, the brand. Toned, long legs that went on for days, a cinched waist, airbrushed pore-less skin, hair polished back into a perfectly swishy pony tail, in pastel pink formal trousers, a matching blazer and an ivory satin top peeking from underneath. She gleaned like a new car.

She had worked so hard to build the picture she saw staring back at her. She looked up at the mirror. It held a different narrative entirely and spoke up now.

Well, they weren't wrong.

Just incomplete.

What AdWeekly didn't know: how Nanki Mehta is also, a secretly greying 32 year old, at a job she could be replaced in a heartbeat in, in a jading marriage that is just about surviving a financial crunch, a pandemic, and losing a grandparent, by the edge of its teeth.

But I guess that wasn't glamorous enough to make the cover *tongue out emoji*'

As she sat mulling this over now, she acknowledged how on most days, even before Covid, she walked this tightrope between the two identities. Clinging desperately onto a powerful workout, a sales report to beat or even just a good hair day to stay on top of it, focussing on the better view of life, while the other followed her around like a shadow just the same.

River popped up on her screen:

Whom do you talk to inside your head?

Whom do I talk to inside my head? Nanki wasn't sure at this moment, but she knew the voice wasn't on her side.

River may have guessed the rabbit hole he sent her down, because before she knew how to respond, he added:

May consider firing said voice.

Sounds about right, she thought as she looked up.

The last shaft of sunlight that lit the room with dust speckling through, was dimming now. The sun was starting to set and it was the part of the day where it was no more evening, but not quite night yet.

The dreaded twilight. Dark but not dark enough, light but barely.

How she hated this part of the day, never knowing what quite to do with herself at this hour.

She dusted off Nanu's books and stacked them neatly back onto the shelf. The pile to be discarded lay scattered on the floor, as she stood up.

His clothes had been folded neatly, after keeping aside the shirts that Dhruv could use.

His medicines, cane and stationery lay in cartons, all set aside to be donated to relevant places.

Nanu's whole life lay wrapped in a few boxes at her feet.

This is it, she thought. Nothing quite like death, to highlight life.

She returned to her phone.

In all fairness, neither is wrong, nor the whole truth individually.

Both are equal parts of the same life.

Ignoring the worse for the better—

is it being optimistic or is it gas-lighting myself?

Wait—are they both the same thing?

Urgh, my brain is doing it again, she thought. Spinning out like a ball of wool, twisting itself into knots.

She went to her home page and saw it from a stranger's perspective. She traced the clues that laid out the map of her life to anyone that looked:

At happy photos; at exquisite souvenirs collected from numerous travels; at shiny awards; at all the signs of the life she had made for herself. At friends, and travels, and family reunions.

Her life clearly laid out in the little boxes of the gram.

The journey between building these tiny boxes and being packed up into the ones that lay at her feet was not that long, and just frankly underwhelming—and *that* was overwhelming.

It's a good life. A great one even. So would this voice SHUT UP?

But the small, defying voice hissed:

Is this all there will ever be?

Evil, *evil* voice.

That black dot. A rip in her fabric of contentment. She could feel it now, knocking.

It was a feeling of a… certain lack.

She typed furiously:

How do you feel a lack?

How do you feel a void?

Numbness is supposed to just be ...numb—

unfeeling and unbothering.

Yet, it is the most bothersome feeling in the world!

She looked back, at her year splayed out in pictures.

Her pretty little life. Insta-sized, filtered just right, decorated with a bow.

It's a lot. And yet, it isn't nearly enough. Meh! Happily ever after is boring, she concluded.

River is typing…

After a moment of Nanki hanging onto her phone, he wrote one line in response to her existential crisis. *One.*

Why is it that people who are so used to the noise of everyday, just wither when forced to listen to silence?

Nanki narrowed her eyes and pulled a face.

Why is it that you answer questions
with even more questions?

Most answers lie in asking the right questions!

Do they not?

She could imagine him chuckling even as she slammed her phone shut. She had had enough wisdom for today.

She allowed herself a deep sigh, and let the burdens of the day, the fortnight, the life fall over her, as she soaked in the city: Noisy, over crowded, buzzing. Alive.

She loved it—and she couldn't stand it a second longer.

10

ON the fourteenth morning, Nanki left for Rishikesh.

She had never travelled anywhere alone. Not without a purpose anyway. Which is why, the last fortnight had felt like a build-up to this point.

Since it was out of character for her, Dhruv, despite grieving himself, had looked rather puzzled.

"B-but why…." his eyes growing bigger behind his glasses with genuine bewilderment. His hair was scruffy and he was due for a shave.

Nanki had had no answer, just a tangible determination. So strong-willed it was too, that it emanated out of her like an odd-kind of defiance. The kind that let him know this was happening, regardless of how he felt about it.

In such an unknown territory he seemed to be, that he agreed to go along with whatever was coming because it was all alien.

"I'm coming with you," he declared.

"Why?" she was calm as a cucumber.

"B-because…!"

There was no end to that sentence, just utter flabbergastion.

"Because what?"

"Because I'm here! B-because you can't go alone!"

Back when they were dating, Nanki remembered how romantic she used to find it for Dhruv to think he needed to protect her. It made her feel *delicate*. It made her feel like a woman—*his* woman.

It felt like a claim to the world, that she was *his* to safeguard.

It took her a couple of years to realise that she wasn't actually in need of any protection. She had learned to love her strength and how she would love to share the pride she felt at having built that. Is that so much to ask for? It had taken her this long to get here after all.

She liked that he thought this was what 'being there for her' meant and how he dutifully extended that emotion, Neanderthal-ish though it was. As they grow older, however, his 'care' will just have to look differently.

The fact was that they were both equally capable. Which should mean that they both protect each other, they both nurture each other, and they both allow each other to grow as individuals—even if that means letting their partnership take a backseat for a little bit.

"Why not?"

"I mean… you'll at least need me to handle things."

"What things?"

"…Nanki!"

Patriarchy had really messed with their heads, hadn't it? What would it take for men to realise that they weren't what's keeping the world together? That they weren't needed at every step, that their permission wasn't asked for.

"Dhruv!" she glared right back.

"You can't just go off alone…" He was repeating himself now, with no rational argument left to make.

"Of course, I can."

"B-but why would you want to?" his voice was getting squeaky. She knew this voice. He felt hurt that she would want a moment in life that didn't include him.

A moment to herself, to figure stuff out in her head without anybody else influencing her decision, even if unknowingly. A moment of silence.

"Because I do, Dhruv. That should be reason enough."

He looked at her like she was putting up a wall between them. A wall that kept him out.

At a later point, she could be more empathetic, but right now, it frustrated her.

Her eyes blazed. Could he *stop* looking like such a wounded puppy?

Wanting a little bit of time for herself wasn't the same as cutting him out.

What was this guilt she was being made to feel at prioritising herself? She didn't stop being an individual just because she signed up to be a part of a pair, did she?

Why do partnerships have to make it so hard to just simply exist as a person? An individual breathing, living person!

Or should she have to want to do everything with him?

Because she didn't.

This was her journey, and he wasn't a part of it. Not right now.

If anything, she needed to know where on the road she was so she can tell him where to meet her!

What about that was so hard to understand?

He huffed incoherent sounds and then, in a resigned, eerily cold tone added, "Let me know if you want me around at all…"

So his modus operandi was going to be anger.

Fine, then.

She could be angry too at the fact that he would be angry.

"I will."

She wanted to take a pair of scissors and chop off his excessively long, unkempt hair. If only he could so much as handle his own grooming, before thinking himself capable of handling her life for her…!

***

She scrolled up to where it began.

The Instagram post of a wildly excited man, as he threw his arms wide open about to take off from the edge of a dizzyingly high bridge painted a canary yellow.

She didn't see a foreigner in him anymore, not even a stranger. Just a friend she had never met.

A friend she hadn't even known she needed.

When it had come to needing space, it had been a no-brainer. Rishikesh had been in too many chats and dreams to not run away to now, when she needed a pocket of earth to unravel, heal and build back up on. To meet River and experience his experience of it. She realised only now that she had never officially responded to that ad. It was a *given* that she wouldn't need to, of course, but for the sake of symbolism, Nanki read the post again:

"Can't wait to experience the world again? We've got something you can hold onto!

Send us your story and why daring to take the last step off the edge is just what you need, and we'll gift you the experience of a lifetime: INDIA'S HIGHEST BUNGY!

In Rishikesh!"

She felt excited at the prospect of walking into that frame soon enough. In the vein of doing things right, Nanki responded to that ad now as she sat in her cab en route to her destination.

It would take her about five more hours and her stomach was rumbling already.

Thank you for giving me a glimpse into something I could look forward to, even while I stayed fraught within the darkest of days. It kept me wading through the turbulent waters in more ways than you will ever know.

I am coming to experience the overwhelm of the edge for myself!

See you soon-ish.

The car trudged lazily along a dusty road for another hour before his response arrived into her DM.

You haven't yet answered WHY you want to dare to Bungy.

Hmph...she thought that much emotion would at least get her some brownie points, let alone endless chats of pouring her heart out to him.

Erm, you know I can just buy it right?

Hahahahha, I do. But I know you won't...

Dammit. He was right.

This was her journey with him. He brought her up to this point, she wanted him to be the one that leads her to the end--right up to the edge.

URGH!!

She grumbled even as she typed it.

It isn't going to be easy.

The first step to finding the answers, is to ask the right questions—remember?

It is a mind game, and it IS mental warfare.

You need to really want to do this.

I need to know your motivations,

your reasons for choosing to enter the battlefield.

I need to know your 'Why'.

You need to know your 'why'.

Is there supposed to be a right answer here?

Never.

Oh Lord! *Fine* then. Here goes...

My motivations, she thought. She thought about this for a while, revisiting her most overwhelming emotions from the last couple of months as she saw River inch closer to the free fall, amidst the lush green mountains.

A LIVER.

He really was one as he jumped, gloriously into the forested valley of Rishikesh.

WHY, she asked herself.

Why did she want to do this that night, and why does she *need* to do it now?

As she asked herself these questions, the words came to her rather freely.

She then wrote her response in a draft, read it, then reread it before hitting send.

Dear River,

You must be right about energy being infectious, because seeing that excitement in you, even from so far away, manages to keep me as curious about such an excitement today

as the day I first laid eyed on this post all those weeks ago.

God, has it just been weeks? It feels like a lifetime ago.

Here's my entry in response to your ad.

My grandfather passed on.

It's odd, I've never phrased death like that before.

A couple of months ago, if I had to share this news, I might have written it as 'passed away', as an ending, but I know better now.

I believe better now.

He has passed on from being contained within an ageing vessel to the infinity he always belonged to.

For that perspective, and for that catharsis, thank you.

As I familiarise myself with death, i find myself attempting to reacquaint with life.

Change is difficult and far too often fears win, courage doesn't feel worth the effort and growth is exchanged for the status quo and curiosity for stability.

But I want to know.

It is time.

I want to know what I'm made of,

I want to face my fears,

I want to to be able to question them, and then

I want to see what I choose.

Just as an observer of my own mind, as a keen stranger to myself.

I want to become aware of myself

so I can be sure of the person I carry on me.

Hopefully somewhere along that road, I'll know God.

That's a meeting I look forward to.

You make faith look beautiful.

I want to know God, the way you know God.

For that, I hope you'll help me meet me.

P.S: I'm on my way.

Regards,

Nanki

The sun was starting to set and the air was getting cooler.

As though on cue, her phone beeped loudly announcing a message from River. It was just one line but it made her heart swell.

Welcome to Rishikesh.

She assumed that to mean she had finally qualified. So much for a freebie, she smiled and shook her head at the wild adventures that awaited her.

The wide concrete roads were tapering off and narrower streets were taking their place. Street lights were coming on and the evening clouds were clearly visible in the absence of the Delhi smog, letting her know that she was nearing her destination.

She rolled the window down and inhaled deeply.

Ah, pure unadulterated oxygen! How had she gone so long without it?

Wind that has whistled through the mountains of the Himalayas and the trees of its jungles just smells different.

She was finally here!

11

It's funny, time had both seemed to have gone by in a blur and also collapsed entirely.

As Nanki got out of her cab at the foot of her camp in Tapovan and stretched herself, she scanned the bustling street that lay before her.

Night had almost fallen, little cafes dotted the landscape, and oh, it was just so nice to see people! Everyday people doing everyday things like all was well. Beautifully mundane, regular life at play. What a sight for sore eyes!

It wasn't quiet by any measure, but the noise had a simpler quality to it, like it was being played out in a single file. The honking of the few cars that chugged along, the humdrum buzz from the shops, the grazing cows in the middle of the road—and the faint roar of the Ganga in the backdrop.

She was tantalisingly close now and she was beckoning: the mighty Ganges, in all her splendour. Waiting for no one yet drawing everyone in anyway.

It had been three years since she had left Delhi. That's over one hundred and fifty-six weeks of the same walls, the same accidental food, the same news. The same hopes, the same fears, the same dreams. Round and round in maddening circles with no exit in sight.

Phew! What a tough road to have made it out of, she sighed half happy, half empty that she had made it.

With a pang, she suddenly missed Dhruv. He would've loved being here. They had been in isolation together, through this sordid nightmare. Now that she was tasting freedom alone, the guilt snagged at her like a knobby old sweater that is all too old and familiar to know exactly where to tug at.

She inhaled deeply and reminded herself of the 'why'. River was right—she would need to hold on tight to this little nugget of introspection.

Earlier in the lockdown, Nanki had missed travelling so much that over a period of time, the desire itself had numbed out to accommodate the new reality. So much so that even while she was on her way here, it hadn't hit her—such a flight of fancy it seemed to be. She only realised how much she had missed it, once she arrived.

Now here, the dull ache of the weeks, the months, the years to break free from the confines of the house came alive as she realised the cage was indeed, behind her.

The sky was hers for the taking.

***

Nanki checked into her tented camp in the late hours of the evening, while the stars created a stunning canopy of their own. There was a little trail leading up to it from the reception. Through the darkening evening, she made her way, dragging her suitcase behind her.

While she had been hastily booking from under the blankets as Dhruv snored softly next to her one night, she came upon this jungle campsite. Its dreamy pictures captivated her like no other lodging had. Beautifully crafted tents amidst what looked like a meadow out of a fairy-tale with wild yellow flowers bursting out of its periphery.

The reality was even better, if that were ever possible in an overly-filtered and glamorised world.

There, right in front of her, towering in a mildly cosy fashion, was her stay for the next few days: Tent #09.

It was an off-white canvas tent, the size of an entire room, covered by an outstretched awning-like cover. An olive green canvas, roll-up window and door adorned the entrance. There was a thick polka dotted fabric on the inside of the roof, adding richly to its rustic vibe. Two little jute chairs stood lazily just outside, perfect for tea-time.

Nanki was so excited, that she almost hopped, skipped and jumped to make her way in, momentarily forgetting to act her age. She rolled up the 'door' like this was all a prop on a movie set and peeked in.

'OH. MY. WOW!' she whispered into the room.

Ah, the inside. It carried the comfort that a steaming mug of hot chocolate did on a winter night.

A yawning bed stood facing her upon a wooden floor, with what must be an attached bathroom at the back. Nanki stepped in to see a little table to her left with a straight backed chair, a comfortable sofa behind it and a little cane cupboard at the other corner of the room.

The entirety of the room was swathed in ethereal white drapes descending down the marquee.

HOW EXCITING! Nanki thought, as she stood amazed.

This must be how children felt when they first sat on airplanes—a sheer curiosity and wonderment.

At what point, do we as adults settle into a pattern of things to repeat instead of chasing the wonders we've never seen and done before? She thought as she brewed herself some hot coffee in the electric kettle.

Although starving, she was way hungrier for soaking up the place than any food.

She decided to drink her coffee by the Ganges, a short walk down the back of the campsite.

As she stepped out, she could feel the icy air fill her lungs leaving them finally satiated. Her breath was fogging up in front of her as she exhaled. Making her way down, she cupped her hands around the mug and let its heat warm her comfortingly. The grass rustled beneath her feet and the chirping of the crickets was drowning out with every step as the gushing river grew louder and louder, until:

Oh my God—there she is!

It wasn't that Nanki hadn't seen her before, but the mighty Ganga had a way of taking anyone's breath away, every single time.

If wild abundance had a face, it would be hers. She flowed with the beauty of an unapologetic woman, unafraid of her power. Making her way through the dense green foliage cascading down along with the mountains that they bedecked, the Ganges had captivated India's heart since the beginning of time.

Mesmerised, Nanki inched closer, unable to pull her gaze away. A built stairway lined this side of the bank and she found a spot to sit on, where the concrete met the river. She plopped herself down and dunked her feet into the freezing water.

Just like that, she became a part of her ripples. The coldness of the water running over her feet and the tangible beauty of the Ganga made it impossible for her to be anywhere else but here. Taking a generous sip of her hot coffee, she realised her mental chatter seemed to have subsided entirely, and she felt a deep calm take hold of her.

To this day, people came here to bathe in this holy water with hopes of washing away all the sins within their lifetime—and in death, to be scattered as ashes for eternal forgiveness and peace.

She pulled her woollen stole in tighter around her.

She could see people burning camphor on a leaf with a marigold flower and floating it away into the river, like a rudimentary boat carrying their hopes and prayers.

The Indian version of a wish upon a star.

All the colours meeting her eyes *felt* more vivid. *Pundits*, robed in saffron, conducted Pujas in small groups, chanting sacred mantras.

Brightly lit temples lined the banks of the river, playing their own hymns amidst a ringing of holy bells. In a lot of ways, all of Rishikesh felt like the inside of a temple.

Pure, holy and blissful.

She brought her phone out and checked for messages: there were none.

It's fine, she told herself and clicked onto Instagram.

Today, the tables would turn.

She clicked the view in front of her and shared a live picture.

From one river, to another...

You've reached!!

I told you the mountains would wait for you.

Them—and its rivers—welcome you home.

Welcome you *hommmmeeee*...! Oh, she could almost cry. Nanki was home indeed.

She felt oddly nervous about actually meeting him. What if he turned out to be crazy—or worse, *ordinary*?

Have you ever wanted something so much
that you can't bear to have it?

Nope, I usually just go in for the freefall *cheeky emoji*

Hahhahaha, quite on brand.

In a pre-covid world, back when life was normal,
I used to spend so much time travelling for work. It was one of
my favourite perks of the job.

That it took me to new places, or newer parts of old places

and I used to *live* for it!

Eventually though, I got so used to it, I started getting tired.
I mean places were just places.

Whenever anyone would ask me what my favourite place was,
I'd say the airport!

I never stopped loving that part.

The wait, just before...
where it could exist in my mind frozen in perpetual perfection.

It was the anticipation of the travel, the idea of a place—
that never got old.

Dhruv used to call it the Airport syndrome.' *☺*

Why, of course! Distance allows the most beautiful illusions.

That is in equal parts, its most wondrous quality as well as its greatest flaw.

Arriving, on the other hand, forces you to engage with the regularity of reality.

What makes you fear it?

I dunno.

Maybe the idea that it won't be as good as I expect it to be.

Or maybe, that it will be, she thought.

Nanki sat there looking out at the mountains that remained hidden within the night. She had waited so long to see them, and she was partly grateful for another night of such a waiting. A dream once realized, is after all, over. The more beautiful it is, the worse it is to be done with.

Staying besotted with a dream

may allow you the kind of reliable happiness one can only ever find in ignorance,

like the prospect of a bonfire does.

Living them, however, will allow you to grow in awareness.

It will keep you in joy, like actually sitting by it, letting it warm you over a long period of time.

Maybe making room for you to spin newer, bigger dreams—now that you're warm and all.

What if it isn't everything you thought it to be?

Then you know.

That it isn't everything you thought it to be.

That the beauty you imagine is only a projection of the beauty within you.

It is only coming *from* you—never the view.

So in that sense, you've been carrying it within you all along.

You just thought you needed an object to project your beauty onto.

Now you can free yourself from that limitation.

Oh, yuk! *cheese emoticon*

She rolled her eyes but smiled nonetheless. He wasn't wrong, but was he ever?

Nanki exited the chat, kept the phone aside and for the rest of the evening, she just let Rishikesh happen to her.

***

The chittering birds delivered a new morning to her.

The night had been cold, her sleep deep, her dreams intense but forgotten already. It took a minute to figure out where she was and she let her mind remind itself gently as she looked around and took the surroundings in.

Nanki had no alarms, no calls, no emails and no plans to get to. This nothing-to-do was as unusual as it was exciting.

She lay staring at the cascading marquee for a bit. She observed how its fabric folded in and flowed down. She could imagine the city start to wake up outside of it.

It felt surreal still, as if she was still seeing it from a distance. So far away she had gone within herself over the last year that even though it was behind her now, the heaviness of its months clung to her like a backpack weighed down by rocks, and its darkness hung like a veil around her.

She was here to unpack, in more ways than one, she decided.

She got out of bed, put on her fluffy fleece foot warmers and walked to the door to roll it up. If she had a limited number of hours here, she'd make them count.

It was early morning still and the sun must've been out but she couldn't see it yet. The fog hung low and clouded away any view beyond two feet. Dew perched itself on the wild shrubbery and every blade of grass in sight. In an hour or two, she'd finally be able to see her beloved mountains.

Going by the icy coldness of the air she inhaled, it felt like Musoorie in the distance would have had snow. If it did, the peaks could be snow-capped!

***

Another hour and a cup of coffee later, Nanki sat curled up with a book she had picked up at the little library in the reception. She stayed buried deep inside a comforter on the jute chairs just outside her tent, lost in its words.

When she looked up, the sun was spilling in magnificent beams through the leaves of the trees around her, warming the meadow. The fog had lifted. It was time!

She almost tripped over the many folds of her shawls, the blankets and the heavy duvet before she managed to get out. Running into the garden, she looked around.

There they were!

The mountains stood tall as ever. Unchanged and majestic.

As old as time itself and as strong as youth.

No photo in the world, no social media in existence could remotely capture the essence of actually witnessing their presence. Of actually *being* here and seeing it in person.

She couldn't believe that she was finally here.

'Never taking travel for granted again…' Nanki muttered under her breath.

An intense gratitude washed over her to be spared a day to be here—another day to be lived amidst such beauty.

Keenly aware of how many weren't, Nanu included, she looked to the mountains, and whispered: *Sorry…*

To an onlooker, it may lack legitimacy, but the mountains knew. They had always shared a language of their own, born of the memories only they were bonded by.

They knew that Nanki was sorry for the years she forgot how much she loved them and for the time she lost in those years to soak up this love.

She was sorry for when she commuted to different places but forgot to truly *travel,* for the curiosity and wonder that had dulled about just how mind bogglingly amazing this world is, of how much there is to see and how little time one gets to see it in …

Most importantly however, and especially in this instant, as she basked in their stoicism, in the knowing that she would forever be as ephemeral to them as a wild flower was to her—she was sorry that she had allowed time to age her.

It wasn't just them that knew her though:

Nanki had been right. They were adorned with pristine snow.

***

An hour later, the campsite had arranged for a meditation session. The last time she pushed herself to meditate, it had been an online session during Nanu's recovery. River had mentioned it too, but she hadn't yet experienced the joy he seemed to get out of it.

Worth a shot, she thought and signed up.

A guru from an Ashram nearby was to come over by 8 am. From that wording, she had been expecting an orange-robed man with his white beard stretching down to his chest. Which is why when a middle-aged Indian woman with a nose ring and her hair in a Shiva knot entered, she had to check herself for her mental stereotypes.

Oh, and they're *blue*... Nanki noticed as this new-age guru unwrapped her muffler off her head, revealing the punky ends of her hair.

She looked to be in her early forties, with a broad, fit build and a warm face. She sported a fitted black tee and those hippie pants with incantations printed all over them—the kinds one only finds in a place like...well, *here*.

She folded her hands and greeted the class of four people that had gathered there:

"Namaste! What a beautiful morning we have here today! I'm Pihu and I'm a certified Yoga instructor. I will be taking you through a half an hour meditative experience today. So how many of you are doing this for the first time?"

One girl, a teenager by the looks of her, at the back raised her hand.

"So all others experts then?" Pihu exclaimed, very happy for no apparent reason.

Nanki waited for others to talk, but the two other men looked around shyly, seeming to have forgotten the mechanisms of language.

"Erm…" Nanki chipped in, with an under confident start on a shaky subject.

"Yes?" Pihu looked to her warmly, raising her eyebrows, inviting the rest of the words in.

"Tried it a bit during lockdown, don't understand it fully, don't exactly get the hype." Her sense of filter had clearly clogged off late, Nanki realised the very second the words had already been spoken.

"What a wonderful reason to join us today then!" Pihu beamed and if it were possible, was even more excited at the possibilities she presented.

Had it been any less beaming a face, Nanki would've assumed it to have been sarcasm, but Pihu didn't seem to have that bone. Nanki smiled back at her with a growing fondness.

"Welcome to our meditation class everyone! Let's sit down in a comfortable position and start with some breathing exercises."

For the next fifteen minutes, they went through the counts of breathing in and exhaling out in double as many counts. A forceful calm had descended upon the little class now.

Pihu perked up again: "The art of breathing is called Pranayama. In Sanskrit, the word 'Prana' means life energy, or life force, and 'Yama' means to poise or control.

"It is the age-old funda of mind over matter—YOU learn to control your breath and master your health.

"Meditation is doing the same dance with your mind. You see, for as long as you are alive, you will breathe anyway, but by understanding the rhythm of your breath, controlling it and disciplining it, you create an equilibrium—a harmonious balance. Similarly, with your mind, your thoughts will run *anyway*. The goal is not to deny them. It is to be okay with their passing while remaining emotionally detached from them.

"Mind chatter can be maddening if not controlled. Hypothetical arguments, ruminating thoughts, rehashing and trying to rearrange old memories, imagining future scenarios—all of it becomes problematic when they hijack your present moments, when it takes you away from noticing the weather touching your skin, the colour of your neighbour's dress, the conversation at the dinner table. It can become scary especially when this mind chatter becomes loud and persistent enough to be out of *your* control.

"We get so caught up in them that we often forget that these thoughts are just thoughts—the potential energy, the seed.

"On their own, they are a mere movie inside your mind! But let it go unchecked, and they can very well wreak havoc.

"Meditation is that tool which allows you to choose which channel you're on and which ones you subscribe to! You choose which of those thoughts are to be made into kinetic energy, flowering that seed into the tree of your life.

"Without that discretion, you'd waste all your water, all your energy and all your precious breath over watering all the weeds too, unknowingly living out of a messy mind. And trust me, there are way too many of those to a highly intelligent and sensitive device like our minds—it picks up all the lint, the voices, the emotions, the energies from well beyond your conscious awareness. *This* is how we sift.

"So, for the next thirty minutes, keep your eyes shut and observe what your mind thinks about when life isn't interfering and let them float past you like clouds. Do not engage, do not process, do not attach to it any of your energy.

"Slowly and with time, as you practice this often enough, you let it lose the strength to draw you in and you start to gain control over redirecting their flow, even when you aren't meditating."

Had it been an orange-robed man with a white beard stretching down to his chest, there is no chance this would have made sense. Pihu made this ancient practice new enough to be able to relate to. In making it relevant, she made it legible.

Now Nanki felt it. She could feel the opening in her heart to genuinely welcome this in.

As she shut her eyes, she let herself free. She could feel her heart start to race when triggering thoughts came up. She watched as hypothetical conversations with Dhruv came up, where her arguments were perfect in everything she hadn't yet in physical reality found the words for. She felt an anxiety flare up about the decisions she was hoping to make and the roads she would be leaving to make them, if she did. She felt terribly about Jeff doing a much better job at her job right now than she was—that was an intolerable thought to live with.

She would just about get drawn into her thoughts, when she would remind herself to detach. She could feel her body relax as her fists unclenched (when had they clenched?)

After what felt like an hour, a cold breeze touched her cheek, reminding her of Nanu's cold hands as he had touched her wrinkles the night before… some memories floated up that lived permanently within the crevices of her mind. Nanu's music filling up the air, the laughter over chai, Dhruv dancing at his door…. then with a jolt, she felt a sense of loss in the pit of her stomach when she thought about going back to a home where Nanu didn't exist anymore.

A terrifying thought floated in. Somehow with Nanu's passing, a glaring question presented itself: if there must be hierarchies of love. Since so much of her sense of 'love' within her marriage was because of Nanu's love for Dhruv and how happy Dhruv had made *him*, now that he was gone, she wondered if her love would be left crumbling through the gaps his absence left behind.

Was her marriage built on some sort of secondary love?

"Love, relax..."

Pihu whispered into her ear, pulling her out of the labyrinthine maze she found herself lost in within her mind, yet again. She must have looked tense. Pihu touched her back, nudging her to sit upright from her now hunched posture.

She was right. It was a jungle of weeds in there.

***

I failed meditation.

One doesn't fail meditation, one finds their way in it.

Oh River...can we chat like regular peasants for once?

Because I really wanted to do it well today.

It was such a beautiful experience.

Early in the day, after I had enjoyed my morning with the beautiful mountains,

with this amazing teacher.

But sitting quietly brought up the worst thoughts,

and before I knew it, I would get entangled within them.

Hahahah! Oh hey, that is part of the process!

Don't be too hard on yourself.

It takes consistently going into the tangles, before you learn to organise them.

Yes, it brings up the worst sometimes,

but isn't it good to know what's lurking beneath the surface?

It's the work that's yet to be done.

Well, it is what I'm here to do...

I'm here to make notes of allll the work that's yet to be done.

This is my first time travelling solo btw.

Oh congratulations!

How is that going for you so far?

I mean, you're never really alone.

The voices in your head keep following you around,

so it isn't as peaceful as I thought

tongue-out emoji

Maybe that's why they pulled you away from any others then?

So you do not get distracted.

Maybe.

You sound like the kind of person who'd wholly and loudly encourage people to travel solo.

Hahaha, actually quite the contrary.

I think one should be *able* to travel alone,

without descending into a feeling of loneliness.

It inculcates an awareness of our own completeness

and an enjoyment of that experience.

Ultimately, we're all going to die alone, aren't we?

That's a skill one must have!

But if one *needs* to, then too it is a cause for concern.

To fall out of touch with yourself amongst people

is as alarming

as not being able to function without them.

That you need to isolate to think and feel and be comfortable means

that you are unable to do that in company.

It's like getting sick from the sun.

If this is going to be the case, you're going to be sick a lot.

Ironically the only way to fix that,

is to strengthen your sense of self to such a degree

that external stimuli don't influence its ecosystem.

This is your emotional immunity.

Try finding happiness outside, when there's tangles within to be resolved and you'll always come up empty.

Keep your insides organised, and the outside will not even matter.

If the lockdown had taught her one thing, it was that. You can have everything perfect on paper and still be far from a fairytale happiness. Believe it or not, it wasn't dependent on the prince finding you, or the crown or the castle, because she found herself all those things and it had still not been enough.

Who knew the search for that happiness would take her through meditation, therapeutic chats and possibly a bungy jump?

12

THE vaccines had been announced. They had been rolled out a month ago, but had only been made accessible to healthcare workers so far—the first responders in this global crisis.

This afternoon, on the little television set in the reception, Nanki saw a reporter standing outside the Ministry of Health in Delhi, announcing that by March, India was ready to start administering the vaccine to its public. It would happen in phases. First to qualify would be the senior citizens and those over the age of forty-five suffering from any comorbidities that left their immunity compromised against the Corona virus.

Wait! This meant—her parents could get vaccinated soon! This was a little doorway to the exit route. They stood a chance—an actual, real chance to be out of this…!

She looked on as all the staff of the camp, having stopped mid-track in their chores to listen in, erupted in applause and relief. Who knew what stories they had to tell?

A doctor came on. He was being asked about his experience with the vaccine. Awkwardly, he narrated his flu-like symptoms that started the night after his shot and lasted for a day. He appealed to everyone to get vaccinated, urging them to help reduce the pressure on hospitals amidst the predictions of a second wave.

"If we don't understand the urgency of this now," he said, straightening his crooked glasses, "our infrastructure could crumble entirely. There will be nothing to save us then."

This was the fastest vaccine in world history to have ever been produced against a virus, and even then, for far too many, it was way too late.

He seemed acutely aware of it too. She looked at how drained he looked. The doctors of the world had been the Army of this war.

"Live a life worth the soldier standing guard on the borders, in the line of fire for your safety," Nanu used to say. He had been a part of India's struggle for freedom and never, ever forgot what he gained—what *we* gained—from the sacrifices of our freedom fighters and soldiers.

The generations to come would also hear of doctors. Of the debt we owe them for risking their lives, safety and mental sanity to walk into hospitals bursting beyond capacity every single day and through way too many nights. They stood guard amidst torrential death, zipping themselves into suffocating PPE kits to treat the country's most contagious patients for the *chance* of some more life to save.

For maybe just another night to make it through, maybe so much as just another breath.

A debt that at the very least, must be worth it, if not repaid.

She looked at the clock hanging next to the TV. It ticked at a quarter past three.

It was almost time.

***

How would I know?

Having rushed back to her room, Nanki was shuffling around, filled with a fervent energy, adding on layers to her already bulky winter clothing. The meeting was scheduled for 4.30 pm in the market area with a Mr Kharbanda from Dharma Foundation. She knew she needed to meet him. What for, she hadn't quite figured out yet.

She threw in a wad of cash to donate, if nothing else. At least she wouldn't have wasted his time.

She felt anxious and tense, realising the incompleteness of her plan only now.

The only thing she could think of was to ask River. She didn't know how to frame her questions to him a minute before she had to leave though. She meant to ask him how she would know what to say and do; how to decipher if this was right for her; how she would know if she must; what value she could possibly bring to the table with her useless skill set in saving the world.

She meant to write further while at the same time, throwing an orange knit scarf around her neck. She was in too much of a flux to type it all. Before she could figure it out though, River had responded already:

By simply asking.

Without possibly knowing it, he had explained it all.

***

An auto-rickshaw had been summoned by a waiter at her camp. As Nanki walked towards it, she noticed how there were no security guards and no CCTVs around the property.

Small towns still held a naive trust in people. They still knew each other by name, they still smiled at passers-by. A little world of its own, frozen in another, simpler time.

Okay, so this has been a while, Nanki thought as she climbed into the little green rickshaw, its engine already revving. The driver had on a mask, and from the rear view mirror gestured with his hand to enquire the 'where to' of this journey.

"Lakshman Jhula Market," she said, and off he drove. The dusty road winded downwards and the auto chugged through it, oddly both rickety but robust at the same time. This is as rudimentary as it gets, she thought as she internally squealed with delight, hidden well under her mask and an unnecessary layer of civilisation.

He dropped her off at the beginning of the street market for thirty rupees. She handed him a fifty and left—the lockdown had been terrible for day wagers, especially those depending on the tourism industry. They lived hand-to-mouth as is and with no income suddenly, it was perplexing to think of how they managed…

The shops lining the road weren't exactly stalls, some had brick and mortar shops behind the open displays out on the road. The sellers stood outside, lazily inviting walkers in. She wanted to just walk around exploring but she had somewhere to be. The shops would have to wait.

A short walk in stood a sudden clearing around a circle. Vehicles weren't allowed beyond this point, and so several bikes and two-wheelers stood parked around it, blatantly ignoring the 'No Parking' sign clearly plastered upon its fence.

Within the circle stood the tall statue of Lord Lakshman, towering over the area named after him, encased in glass. The crossbow in his hand, the pack of arrows on his back, his royal yellow dhoti, the Rudraksha beads tying his hair into a knot and his chest inflated with pride was just as she remembered it. Iconic in its simplicity. Even though she should hurry onward, she couldn't help stop a second longer to admire it.

With a jolt came the realisation that this was the first time ever that she was seeing it without her family.

'If only I could see it a little more, on their behalf…. to trap this feeling in little gift boxes to carry back to them', she thought.

She checked her phone. 4.12 pm. It was supposed to be here somewhere.

She looked around and spotted the landmark he had given to her. 'Pooja Bhandaar', a little store of religious supplies stood at the back right corner of the statue. A narrow road slipped past it, very missable if one didn't know to look for it.

She walked down it till she came upon the cafe tucked away to the left. A chalkboard-stand outside announced its name: 'Chai Library'. She walked closer to the salon with exposed bricks and an olive green doorway. She pushed it open. A door chime tinkered above as she did and the smell of masala chai and freshly baked sweet buns wafted thickly through its air.

She looked around her. He wasn't here yet. The only light came from the yellow bulbs hanging low. The counter stood right opposite her, with the wall behind it covered in blackboard, listing out at least fifty types of teas in white chalk, with masala chai standing out in orange. *Had* to have a place of privilege, this OG.

This place had no view and it didn't bother with it. They converted the linear space to the left of the counter into a corridor library with floor-to-ceiling bookshelves running across the back wall and tables of two set across. The dim lighting, the wooden panelled floors lent it the vibe of an almost-boudoir, save for the smell of whiskey and some jazz in the background. Instead, there were low Rishikesh hymns and the smell of chai and somehow it would seem that this worked just as well.

She asked for some water and waited. Another fifteen minutes must have passed before the door tinkered once more and a black turbaned man walked through it. He had on a mask so it was hard to tell if it was the one who matched the Whatsapp DP of his contact card. Familiar with his way around, he looked to the corridor and upon spotting her, made his way to the table.

"Namaste-ji. Nanki Mehta?" folding his hands, he enquired. She stood up and nodded, folding her hands to greet him just the same.

He was a tall, stately man, looking to be in his sixties, dressed formally, in a coat and everything. He gestured her to sit down and thankfully, started: “Bete, first, what will you have?”

Bete, meaning child. It had been a couple of days since she had been called that endearment—since Nanu, to be precise—and felt irrationally overwhelmed. She cleared her throat to pace herself and said: “I-I was thinking of trying their nettle tea. I have never heard of it.”

“Oh, you know there’s a place here where they make soup out of stinging nettles too!” There was a twinkle in his eyes and a bounding, wondrous joy to his deep voice.

“Oh, that sounds absolutely bizarre. I think I want to try it!” she replied, as he took his mask off, revealing a kind face, mostly covered in a greying beard and a moustache that curled up at the edges. If Santa Claus were real… he’d have tough competition in the jolly department.

He placed the order, with a kulhad chai for himself and a plate of onion pakoras and mini samosas for the table.

She felt like a child in his company, being ordered for of all the flavours of candy in a sweet shop.

He clasped his hands onto the table and looked her directly in the eye, “Yes, so. How may I be of help to you?”

“Sir, I just wanted to thank you for the tremendous work you’ve done during the pandemic. We could save a member in our neighbourhood only because of the tireless work of one of your employees. I don’t think there are enough words to cover it…” her voice trailed off.

He folded his hands again. “God must be happy with us to have worked through us, bete. Thank you for letting me know.”

“I was wondering…” she began and didn’t understand where to

take it. "Like, what is your process? What is it that you do and how can others be a part of it?"

"Yes, of course! I am Veer Kharbanda, this organisation Dharma Foundation was started by me about a decade ago now.

"We started very small. Just got some children from our colony to volunteer in collecting leftover food from the houses to distribute among street kids. We wanted to inculcate an awareness among them of what they can do with their privilege and of course have a responsible way of consuming our resources instead of just throwing it away while so many slept hungry. The food could not be half eaten, stale or rotten in anyway. It was fresh food that had gone untouched. The children went up to every house to collect it, carrying disposable boxes to pack it in and then walked through to the market area, distributing it to the needy.

"Eventually, families started waiting for the kids to show up. Some prepared food specially to give to them—even sweets around festivals! It was a very enriching experience for everyone involved, but it petered out when exam time came around and we had to stop.

"Our gated community however, had gained some momentum. A couple of the families put their heads together and decided upon registering ourselves as an NGO*. I took charge of the planning and handled it thereon. At the time, I was working a job, with a few years left for retirement. After that though, this became my full time thing—Ah, yes."

The food had arrived. Her steaming water-based green leaf tea in a white mug, his saffron spiced milk tea in an earthen 'kulhad'. The piping-hot snacks came on a wooden platter. She picked one bite-sized samosa up and looked at him to go on.

"These are a specialty here," he smiled as she took a small bite. Freshly out of the fryer, burning hot inside and lip-smackingly

* Non-Government Organization

delicious, these samosas were truly exceptional. With spicy mashed potatoes and—raisins? What a weird, weird combination. Perfection, actually.

He smiled at her befuddlement and went on.

"Our core team is still four members from our neighbour families from back then."

"Just four?" This was surprising. They had been all over the media, doing so much work during the pandemic with pictures showing groups of helpers wearing black tees with 'Dharma' printed over it. She had imagined it to be a full-fledged organisation.

"Yes actually. The others are volunteers. While we have some ardent volunteers who provide us with almost stable service, only four are permanent 'employees' within the organisation. Others come and go as their time and will permits. We started with putting in our own money but to scale up we rely on donations. Every contribution goes a long way but they are wavering. Most NGOs depend heavily on this erraticism as their main source of man and money power. It's what keeps us in existence. However, it isn't always stable. Barely ever, in fact."

"That must be difficult..." she had come here thinking how she could eat a piece of their altruistic cake. What she could learn about baking it and what she could take away. Instead, she came upon another realisation rather quickly: It hadn't struck her that they could need help too. Whoever thinks about the givers? They are already ample enough to be giving unconditionally, what could they possibly be given to?

And that's how they're the first ones to starve, she thought.

"Yes, it is. When we started this, our hearts were full and we thought we could run on its fumes. That's both, the beauty and folly of youth.

"We were neither entirely wrong nor right. Just incomplete in our understanding. We did run on its fumes, but there's only so far one can go without fuel. No matter how much you do, there's always more to be done. We had to get smart about what we are capable of and accept that which we can't.

"Over a period of time however, while our hearts remain just as full, there is this keen awareness that one can't depend entirely on passion. In fact, the most aware of this fact will be the people who have tried to. It needs consistency, direction and means to become a breathing, living entity."

She winced suddenly in disgust. She had taken a swig of her nettle tea and it tasted a lot like… *spinach.*

"Don't know what I was expecting," she explained as he stopped suddenly, startled, "but it wasn't *that!*"

He threw his head back and roared with laughter. "What else will you have, bete?"

She looked down at her cup, it was just a few more sips of terrible tea. "Oh, it's fine, Sir…"

"Nonsense! Life is too short for 'fine'. Never settle for anything less than spectacular!" He motioned the waiter to the table.

It must be the mountains, she thought, that didn't just stop at making poets out of everyone—it made poetry out of its people too.

"Okay then, I'll have what you're having," and another kulhad chai was ordered…

She took out a notepad and dashed some bullet points on to it.

- manpower
- money
- stability

"We officially started with a free tuition for underprivileged children. They didn't go to schools and a lot of them didn't even want to. It was a waste to them, they needed to earn.

"So we started with teaching them to simply read and write. Slowly it grew into a small learning centre where we teach them life skills they can use for vocations that don't require a qualification; we run that to this day, but most of our notable work was actually ad hoc; we would extend ourselves during any crisis we could help with. Like the Kerala floods, the Rishikesh landslides, Bihar earthquakes and now Covid.

"We had made a good name for ourselves within our locality and they would trust us with diverting their donations. The wonderful thing was, during such disaster management initiatives, our students from our learning centre, and even their older family members were more than willing to take the training to volunteer with the relief work on ground. This included a two day course on first-aid and an orientation on the flow of operations that we would organise before dispatching them to the hit-zones."

"What a fitting full circle..." Nanki said.

The people that received kindness were the first ones to volunteer to give it, because they *knew* what that meant. River was right; energy was infectious. No wonder people treat people the way they have been treated.

Hurt people *hurt* people; loved people *love* people.

It was so important then, for those well-loved to reach out to others with the love inevitably contained within them. They have this precious, *precious* currency that way too many are empty of.

It's one thing to sit in your corner and be a kind person when spoken to, it's another to go out there and give it. All that love bottled up inside does no good to the world, does it?

If only one could find it in themselves to start that domino effect.

"So you have no singular mission?" Branding-wise, this made them weak, a lack of a USP.

"Just to give what we can. Is that not singular enough?" he had a twinkle in his eye.

She smiled back. It should be.

"Our mission, like people and life, isn't two dimensional. Its richness lies in its complexities. It holds layers and like water, flows where it needs to."

"Beyond your locality though, how do people know of you? Like during Covid, you were huge. In the papers and on social media and everything. I actually thought your NGO only catered to providing oxygen cylinders. I had no idea the amount of work that you have accomplished in the past. How did you manage that when it hasn't been your forte?"

"That's simple. It isn't because we were experts, it's because we were *there*. Showing up when people were desperate. Times were tough and no one had the luxury of choice nor time. You know, it is the easiest during a crisis to get volunteers and donations.

"Visible misery sells fast. We genuinely were never wanting for money or workers during that period—we had an abundance of both. People were wanting, even desperate to help because we were all suffering. Nothing binds people together more than common pain.

"We were restricted by a genuine shortage of resources, as was everyone. We were merely trying to organise its flow of operations in the best way possible to optimise it. It's when it is not an emergency that we have trouble running the show. Misery still exists, it's just not urgent enough nor visible enough to be tended to."

She scribbled into her book:

- Visible misery
- sustainability.

How does one make consistent pain be felt consistently enough to inspire sustainable support? It is natural to numb out anything that is too consistent. How is pain kept fresh and alive?

"In Sikhism, we believe in 'Dasvandh'-that is setting aside one tenth of our income and life energy towards Seva. In my experience, everyone wants to contribute, they want to help. The loss, more than in a lack of means, lies in passivity. It's only in times of need that people sit up and take stock of what is needed and appreciate and support the givers. Otherwise, it's taken for granted, unnecessary even. Our spirits must never tire of action. What would be the difference between being alive or not, then?"

The darkness was growing outside but Nanki felt comforted by his light. She thanked him for his time.

Before they left though, she blurted out, "Why did you agree to meet me?"

She really couldn't help herself.

After all, it had just been a call a month ago enquiring generally and then one more, to Mr Kharbanda directly this time, a day before she left for Rishikesh, scheduling the day and time. She had only said she wanted to thank them for saving a life that had mattered to her. That she would love to know more of what they do. There was nothing he stood to get out of his time with her and yet unhesitatingly, he had agreed.

On their website they had listed their locations as Gurugram, Chandigarh, Jaipur and Rishikesh. She had called and asked to meet their Rishikesh team. It turned out, the founder *was* the Rishikesh team and he visited often on account of his son working in a rafting company here.

Delhi was listed as their head office but she didn't want to meet them there. It was a different segment in her mind, a different life which demanded a different her.

Here? Now here, she could be born again. She could choose to be whomever she wanted to be.

Mr Kharbanda paused before he answered, "Because I sensed something in you."

"What was that?" she tilted her head, waiting.

"A seed…and an urgency to break out of it."

Yep, she thought as they stepped out into the cold yet again and watched him walk away.

Ridiculous optimists, that's what saves the world in the end.

13

It had been three days of glossing over the notes from her meeting with Mr Kharbanda. Staring at the same bullet points until a solution, an idea, a picture started to form out of them but it was one she was bent on suppressing. This was harder than Nanki had imagined. It was all she could see and had no more sight to spare.

It came from who she had been, a version she was trying not to be anymore, and that just won't do.

This evening, Nanki sat with the same notepad over a bonfire that the camp put up every night in their lawns, the pencil poised over the paper, waiting. She wasn't writing what was coming to her and different just...wasn't.

The teenage girl from her Yoga class was sprawled on the hammock across from her, as she was every other evening, with her headphones on and music seeping out of it. Not loud enough to annoy others, but definitely loud enough to burst her own eardrums while staying perpetually glued to the bulky headset. Nanki didn't tell her that though—she would not cross that bridge into the old-people category. She just *wouldn't.*

The two other men from the class must have checked out already. They had travelled together from Amritsar, as had been discussed just that morning, after their daily meditation session. Now, *those* had been going rather well. The four of them and Pihu had become more comfortable with the silence and with the journey of getting lost in it alone but together. They shared pleasantries, enquired about the wellbeing of those back home and not too much else, each dealing with their own drama, each here for an escape.

She was looking at the twinkling stars for *any* inspiration when her phone buzzed. It was Jaya.

Her immediate reaction was to scrounge for any reason she could use as an excuse later to not pick up right now. She couldn't find one.

"Hello…" she started sheepishly. The conversation hadn't even begun, and she was apologetic already. There was no point playing dumb with Jaya: she knew too well her level of perceptiveness. She had crafted it after all.

"My dear girl…" Jaya began curtly. *Oops*, she was in trouble. Nanki paced herself.

"First, you go MIA.* I didn't say a thing assuming you need the break to grieve Nanu. Then I find out from *Dhruv* that you've taken off to Rishikesh in the middle of a pandemic. Care to explain to me what's going on in that head of yours? Care to explain to *him*?"

Nanki narrowed her eyes. So Dhruv and Jaya had had a chat….

She stayed silent. "Nanki! This is enough. It is not everyone's job to guess your next step. You are accountable to your work, to your husband and to me. I know times are tough but they're tough for everybody. Adult up!"

"I'm sorry." Her tone was flat. This wasn't a lie but it was not nearly the whole picture.

"That's it? You were given the opportunity of a *lifetime*—that I'm still stalling for you by the way. God knows how I'm doing it. God knows how terrible it is looking that the person who is supposed to lead a brand, isn't even present during its painstaking creation…"

"Jaya, I'm not going to do it."

* Missing in action

Until that point she hadn't even realised that her mind was so made up.

There was a silence.

"Excuse—WHAT?"

"I'm not doing it," she repeated. She didn't know if this was a break or if this was a resignation. She just knew she had no mental bandwidth to lead an account, much less to be pressured into urgent action because it was due to hit the markets in a few months. She was done being obligated to things she never chose and she was done being rushed through life with a pace that wasn't her own.

"Why. The hell. Not? Do you think opportunities like these fall from trees?"

Nanki stayed silent because there was nothing to say that made any rational sense. Even to her. Except that her heart was elsewhere and she had to find where it was taking her. That would just have to be enough.

Jaya started on a rant, stating everything she knew already. "... You stopped responding to emails..."

Nanki muted herself and let her rant away to her heart's content, holding the phone at a distance so she could hear the fire crackle and breathe without being interrupted.

"...The team is working round the clock because this is *such* a big account for us..."

The teenager flung her feet down and sat looking at her. They locked eyes and she smiled.

"...Do you have any idea what you're doing Nanki?" Jaya blasted.

To allay her anxiety at feeling cornered, Nanki, while still on mute, mindlessly asked the teenager instead:

"How can you *ever* hear your own thoughts through that?"

Oh *damn*. Okay then, that bridge had officially been burned down.

"I CAN'T! That's the whole point." she yelled over the noise.

Well, Nanki shrugged. That was probably the difference between the pains of growing and the pains of having grown.

The former is about shutting up the maddening inner voice for a moment of peace—a desperation to get off the carousel; the latter is an agonising struggle to find it, like it is the only thing that could save you from flying off of it. What is common is the desperation to survive the circus.

She unmuted herself, drew the mobile close to her and finally spoke into it.

"Not a clue."

And for the first time in a really long time, she was okay with that.

14

"SLOWLY, you may now open your eyes..." Pihu stood with her hands on her hips, the sun hanging behind her head like a halo.

It was starting to warm up, if only a tad. Nanki felt a deep peacefulness within her. This was her fifth session in a row and she felt mighty proud of herself. Meditation was still a struggle but she looked forward to the journey now. The jungles were rife but they didn't feel dangerous anymore.

As Pihu starting packing up to leave, she left the students to languish as they will. Nanki didn't feel like moving yet. She sat there in a half Padmasana, or the lotus pose, touched her fingers to the blades of the grass and enjoyed the feel of them. This was an idyllic life, a background of mountains, the sensation of the earth below, the sound of the gushing Ganga.

"So I don't know if you know...we have the Kumbh Mela coming up in about a month." Nanki looked up from her reverie to see Pihu pensively address the class. The teenager was still here and another family of four from Dehradun had checked in and joined them today.

"Try as we might, we can't seem to stop it. It is being touted as a 'super spreader'—and boy, that doesn't even begin to cover it. If you all plan to be here long, I would suggest to keep it short of that. Rishikesh and Haridwar will become Covid hotspots and no amount of precautions can really prevent that. Peeps, the whole country may be hitting into a second wave as it is. You don't want to be locked out of your states and definitely not here with the millions of pilgrims thronging the Ganga for their holy bath."

They shared nervous glances and nodded solemnly.

The Kumbh Mela, a Hindu festival, happened once in twelve years amidst a cycle of places and had an ardent audience of its own. It invited way too many congregations from the farthest ends of the country to take a dip of atonement in consecrated waters for a global pandemic but as it were, religion in India could not be messed with, least of all with logic.

So a *month*. An end date had been served and a month was as far as she could be here. She had to arrive at the end of her road before the trip came to its.

An urgency kicked in. She brought out her phone and hopped onto River's DMs.

She started to write and then deleted her messages. She didn't need to have a chat on text anymore. They could meet in person!

Hi River.

She ventured slowly, wondering if he thought of her as friend enough to meet outside of the bridge. So far, he had only been the Jump Master and she, a person with fears. It was, she assumed, *natural* for him to gravitate towards them and take the time to sort through each one of its shades to lead her up to the point of climax—the edge. After that, she was on her own.

But friends? Who knew if he felt *that*. All Nanki knew was that without his element of friendliness, his guidance would have meant a lot less. It is what made her trust him.

Well, this was pretty much the same thing, all meshed into one odd relationship.

Hello Nanki :)

You sound like you must be finding your way back into your skin...

Sorry?

Oh you know.

This is the first time you've said Hi.

Not with thoughts wandering off the edge of the earth,

not with emotions threatening to take you under,

just peacefully present to this moment.

Just... Hi.

Was that true? How could it be?

I guess I am.

Finding my way back into my skin.

Would you care for a coffee while I navigate the rest of the route?

She hoped he wouldn't assume it to be a date. *God*, she thought, please don't be cheesy.

How about your Bungy jump?

Oh, thank God.

I'm not ready for my jump yet.

I'll arrive at the edge—when I arrive at the edge.

It will have to be soon, before the Kumbh Mela, in fact,

because I must leave by then.

But it isn't now.

There was a moment's pause. Then—

I'm more of a masala chai person

Nanki laughed out loud.

I know just the place...

Oh, have you tried the nettle tea here?

That's when Nanki exited the chat but sent a rolling eyes emoji before she did.

***

They were to meet by six-thirty pm at Chai Library.

Nanki wandered through the market as the lights started coming on. The street hawkers had tied strings of bulbs to their carts that twinkled magically now. Tantric music of Sanskrit hymns sung in exotic foreign accents clung to the air that carried them along with the smell of incense.

She made her way to the cafe for the second time in less than a week. She felt surprisingly nervous about this one—jittery almost.

For a stranger, he knew too much about her. Now that he was stepping outside her phone texts and becoming a real, living human, she felt uncomfortably...*seen*. She was also, however, excited to see *him*.

She pushed the door open and entered to the familiar jangling of the door chimes; the dim yellow lights flooding the place looked even brighter in contrast to the darkening evening outside. She looked around—he was already here!

River sat on the farthest table at the end of the library corridor, in a big, dark blue jacket, pouring into a hardbound book. Skin almost glowing under his brown dishevelled hair: this was the face she had imagined all through her lockdown as the face of a LIVER.

Nanki walked slowly up to him. He looked up from his book only when she was just two steps away. For the length of a heartbeat, he had an entirely blank expression. Nanki inhaled sharply as she looked at him; his eyes were a shade of blue one would imagine the bottom of the ocean to be made of, where the light didn't even reach but held a terrifying calm of its own.

In the next second, as his eyes met hers, his face broke into the widest smile Nanki had ever seen on a human—and he had dimples!

Oh, just so much beauty is lost in translation from reality to the digital, Nanki thought, her own smile mirroring his now.

He stood up—more like unfurled himself. He was much taller than Nanki had imagined—and walked around the table with his hands outstretched for a.... *handshake*. He hunched down ever so slightly to fit into her eye-line and extended a very warm handshake with both his hands clasping hers, that felt more like a formal, courteous version of a hug.

"*Namaste* Nanki!" *Oh boy*, she had had no idea what his voice sounded like. It was warm as the *sun*, and heavenly accented.

"Bonsoir, River!" her voice a tad squeaky. He chuckled and pulled out a chair for her.

"Ah alors tu parles français?" River invited her in playfully as he sat himself down.

"Okay, no. That's all I had." He laughed a laugh that would light up the galaxy.

The next fifteen minutes went by in a blur of nervous chatter. She asked him about his day and he replied with "The usual! Got a couple of people to Bungy, that is all!"

"Riiight, the *usual*."

Nanki pointed at an 'I've Got Guts!!!' badge on his black T-shirt and he explained, "Oh! Company policy. All our crew who've jumped wear it. We also give it to the jumpers after their Bungy, so hopefully it will be yours soon! We are seeing fewer people in Rishikesh now that the cases are rising again..."

Nanki started easing up and River felt like River again. Not the detached human his physical presence seemed to display, but as her own friend-*ish* person she had come to think of him as.

The waiter came to the table to take their order and Nanki asked him for recommendations. She decided upon a Butter Tea, a specialty from the Himalayas. It was, he explained, also known as Gur-Gur Chai, made of tea leaves from Ladakh, yak milk butter, water and salt.

River, after careful deliberation, picked a Kashmiri Noon Chai—a sweet milk tea brewed with cardamom, salt and—baking soda?!—which apparently lent it a distinctive pink colour.

Nanki resumed, "This place…is *whacky*. Lived in India all my life and had no idea we have SO many teas."

River let out a sunny chortle. "It's crazy how we numb out to things the more they are in our face—the more you see of it, the lesser you truly *see* it."

She knew he wasn't just talking about the teas. "Well, yeah! But it is how it's designed to be, isn't it? It is kinda vain though, you know. Like if I was God, I'd design it differently."

He looked up, taken aback. Then he cut straight to the source of this intensity "How are things back home?"

"I don't know," she said. It was an honest answer. He sat back silently, exuding a most calming patience, waiting for her to go on. "Thank God for you though! I don't know how—or why—you were always there, but…it was a lot."

A part of Nanki gagged, at her bleeding emotion *again*. How it would've disgusted her a few months ago, and even now, she hoped to revert to that comfortable detached-*ness* soon. Everyone was so openly vulnerable all the time, *Gawd*.

River shook his head, "Oh pff…I was a workaholic on forced sabbatical. Rishikesh was on lockdown too, of course. It was no bother. In fact, by looking to me to lend you courage—you allowed me to be a Jump Master, even without my bridge. Who would've thought my profession would take this form?"

Hmmm. That…happened later though, Nanki thought. Eventually.

"Why did you start? Why did you allow me into your space? I could've been any creep."

Their teas arrived and the question hung in the air. The Noon Chai was indeed a pretty mild hue of pink, served in a wide-rimmed glass cup with pistachio flakes and dried rose petal garnishes. River eyed it with a childlike fascination as it was placed in front of him. Nanki's Butter Tea came in a floral bowl with jaggery cubes on the side. So far it looked like regular tea and had no quirky garnishes to talk about. A basket of complimentary sweet buns was placed on the table with a gracious smile by the waiter.

"Oh, what fun!" River exclaimed. The teas were steaming hot and Nanki cupped her hands around hers.

"Well?" Nanki probed.

River smiled but his energy shifted. He put his cup down and looked out the window before answering.

"I was returning from the hospital that night. I had lost a friend to Covid. I couldn't go to him, because they weren't allowing access to bodies of Covid patients. So I drove to where I needed to instead.

Within the mountains, I am home. It was easy to understand that...*want* in you because I was there too. I couldn't imagine making it through that without them. It was the least I could do."

Her heart dropped to the floor. She realized how little she knew about him, though she still and inexplicably felt sure of knowing the essence of him.

'Within the mountains, I am home.'

River. Come to think of it, what French man is ever called River? She wondered if it was a self-chosen stage name. The role he embodies as a Jump Master in Rishikesh. She didn't dare ask though. She wasn't ready to trade the myth of him just yet.

It didn't even matter in fact. He was who he chose to be.

She only felt gutted for not even having offered a human-to-human connection and making a God of him instead. "Why didn't you tell me that?" she whispered.

He smiled now, coming back into his own, "Ah, it was too much to get into, I guess. I wished then that I had a pocket of earth that could just pour into me without needing an exchange 'coz I had nothing to give right then. So I became that to you. When you're that depleted, all you need is to become full of you."

To become 'full of you'—has such a negative connotation in colloquial English, Nanki pondered. Clearly unknowing of it, River said it unhesitatingly. And oh so beautifully.

Of course, one *must* become 'full' of themselves. Up to the brim and bursting through the seams. What the hell else are they supposed to be full of?

Nanki sipped on her tea. An unusual version of buttery goodness made its way down her throat. Not overly rich, not really weird either, this was a warm, cosy blanket in a mug that one snuggles under after a long day out in the cold. She plopped two cubes of jaggery in, because *why not*.

"Don't you need friends too?" Nanki reached out. Better late than never.

"I do, and I have them. Why do you ask?"

Ouch. He didn't think of her as his friend though he allowed her *her* illusion of him. But they weren't exactly friends, were they? Which just goes to prove that not every meaningful connection had to be a friendship. A term too loosely used now.

"Oh, we need more labels to define human relationships, don't we?"

"Oh I think we need far lesser," River smacked his lips, gulping down a generous sip, "Labels limit things."

Hmm. She had decided. Whatever this was, *was*. Labels or not, it was, as she had said, a *lot*.

“That’s why it works. By thinking of me as different than them, is why people trust me with more strength than them. We equalize the things we know. And to think of something as equal is to assume it to suffer from our own failures. Some people are builders in this world. They take any landscape and build it into a new whole. Some people are so whole themselves, they become a function of giving. These are the teachers and the givers. Even at their broken down pieces, they’ll still find something to give.

Some, like me, are facilitators. We work best by remaining incomplete to the ones we hope to facilitate to. So incomplete in fact, that by filling the gaps in your knowledge, you raise me up to a figment of your own imagination.

That’s how you see the version you seek.

I am nothing. I am simply what you need. So you can become whole again.

Which by default makes me *everything*, but that’s an ego trip I’ll take another day” he said, winking.

After all this time, he was still a stranger but he was also anything but. She had always known this but hadn’t verbalized it in so many words. No point denying it now. It was a terribly kind gift, so she must make the most of it.

“Actually, you’re right. And this makes you what… a lowkey therapist?”

“Naww, I’m too underqualified for that. I’m…maybe just the devil’s advocate. An argument for another perspective. A Jump Master getting you to jump” his eyes twinkled.

Nanki held his gaze as she ran her finger around the rim of her cup. Witnessing his mind in person felt like stumbling upon impromptu poetry.

“So. Again. How are things back home?” this time, River probed.

Now, she was willing to venture into this question for she had no more for him. She looked around her.

Simply choosing to be here because she wanted to—and making it happen, felt like a victory. River sat across from her, like a symbol in himself, of what lay ahead of her. It was like a *gathering* of courage for what was to come. However, the guilt about what it was costing her stayed within her, and followed her wherever she went. It came to her in waves, wearing different faces at different times.

She felt at peace right now though—and only because she did, did she allow herself to consciously revisit what she had left behind. If only to detangle the various threads that kept her heart in knots, she allowed River into the gaps between their messages.

She told him about Jaya, who had brought her up in her career like a parent does in life. Nanki wasn't naive, she knew she was an *investment,* that would probably end up bearing no return for her, if she followed her heart instead of Jaya's vision.

Then, she conjured up for him the befuddled face of her husband Dhruv, who was trying his hardest to bring everything back to where it was before Covid, and couldn't understand why instead of holding on to their 'normal' after such a nightmare, she would want to let go of it entirely.

Sometimes, she told River, her guilt held the angelic face of Kavya, which for some reason in her mind now, was burned with sorrowful tears. That face ...the one that started it all.

Then—and this was difficult—there was the unconditionally loving face of Nanu, who, right up to the end, saw her as the woman she hoped to be.

If she didn't become her, *that* would be her biggest failure. Possibly the only one that really counted.

She looked at him watching her keenly. From the bulb hanging over her head, the ocean in his eyes glistened, mirroring back a reflection:

And then there was *her*.

She didn't say that aloud but he understood. He held her gaze allowing her a moment to let the weight of that thought tide through.

She then told him about Mr Kharbanda and his inspiring work, her meeting, her inexplicable pull and her search for answers to questions she was stumbling upon as the days went by.

This entire monologue surprisingly took no more than twenty minutes. It is only a little while that can seem to eat up all of life sometimes.

"So what do you do now?" River asked her.

"Well, that's what I'm yet to figure out..."

"In my experience, when one doesn't know the answers, it's because they're usually trying to guess someone else's. Betraying their instincts, they're caged within someone else's world."

"Okayy...?" Nanki looked at him a second and wondered if that's what she was doing. She got out her notepad mindlessly, looking for clues. She *was* trying to guess others' answers. Dhruv's, Mr Kharbanda's, Jaya's...God's. Trying to imagine what they would deem as the *best* answers and fighting to guess it.

Where she knew she strayed away from *their* best answers, she felt it as an angst in the heart of her chest. But none of their answers matched of course. In fact, most were conflicting. Caught in the crossfire, *her* life was becoming a stagnating dilemma.

Oh my *God*, she gasped. It was...probably not her emotion at all! Could it be....that it was the angst she anticipated *them* to feel and carried them on their behalf, burdening her, weighing her down.

Eventually it was that weight that was distancing her from them all so she could have a moment of lightness.

Nanki gathered herself. She went over the points again, aloud this time, for River. His fingers lingered on her scribble of 'visible misery' and she explained what Mr Kharbanda had meant. The struggle to keep pain fresh and alive enough to stay hurting. He smiled.

"Humans are too adaptable for their own good" Nanki said and gave in to one of the sweet buns herself. Sprinkled with colourful tutti-fruttis, it reminded her of childhood

"Isn't it ironic, that it was 'adaptability'—our ability to adjust into our surroundings, modify ourselves to fit into our environment, to grow numb to what is intolerable and painful so we can persist through it—that got us to survive, and ultimately, it will be adaptability that will kill us.

"We always found a way to adapt to what was killing us in order to survive, when the pain *should* have been felt instead, for *it* to be okay. That would be the bigger game."

Huh. Wasn't that true.

"What've you thought about it, then?" he asked gesturing to the notepad.

"Oh, I haven't been a fan of my brain off late." She brushed it off, since that was the question she had been both evading, and trying to address herself. "I am, in fact," with mischief dripping into her tone, she added, "here to birth a new one. Isn't that what your edge is for?"

He gave out a hearty laugh before looking down at his now empty cup.

"Ah, the edge…" he spoke the word slowly and with a lovingness only a poet must evoke for his muse.

"But that would mean you'd have to kill the old one? I'm sure any head has only space for one!"

“Mmm, that wouldn’t be the worst thing in the world” she said with a twinkle in her eye.

“So losing yourself will make the world a better place somehow? Huh…” River was mentally testing this theory. A moment later, confusion writ all over his face, he said “I don’t see how you justify life by that, when you are on a mission to die by default. Stifling *your* unique perspective is as good as not being present to your experience. Trading that for a mere *concept* of goodness…its dis-in-genuous.” He said the word slowly, like it had taken a lot of practice to learn it.

River had a counter question, which were usually his best answers, “If you could be great, at the cost of being happy, would you choose it still? And would that be a valid choice—the *better* choice even?”

Nanki had been over this in her head, “Maybe all the great people to have ever lived, *did*. And that’s probably how they earned their happiness.”

What a cruel joke existence seemed to be to have played into. Jaya, her career, the life she planned with Dhruv—all of it was the life that she had built for herself.

So now, just because she was *feeling* like rethinking it, she should give all of it up, deeming it to be divinely ordained?

That was how disposable her plans should be to honour innate volatile desires?

That was self-love? That was prayer?

Either that, or one stays miserable within oneself?

“It is,” she said, “The divine blackmail : ‘Keep Flowing, or else…”

River sighed.

“So after everything, you’re finally giving in to that black hole in the end. Allowing it to consume you and deciding that to be the better existence.”

The black hole. The tear in her fabric of existence. The disconnect.

She mulled this over now, and repeated in her head, 'If you could be great, at the cost of being happy, would you choose it still? And would that be a valid choice—the *better* choice even?'

Before she could process the thought, River went on, "It's funny, jumpers always go in thinking the conflict is between what lays ahead of them or behind: the fear of the height in front or the safety of the ground behind them: when in fact its about the will of the person straddling the middle. Do they let the outside get in or do they allow their insides to erupt outwards—that is the whole sport.

Oh, we ourselves are our greatest blind spot. We only register what we can see and perceive and sense and we can't do any of those with ourselves, until we *really* look hard enough to see the most obvious. To see what we have grown most unseeing and numb to:

I can see you, I can't see me. I only know me though—not you at all, not outside of my perception anyway, but do I trust that knowledge? Till I don't learn to, you keep filling me up but I keep drowning myself out.

God…was a smart cookie after all. You had to learn of giving, I agree, but it had to go through you."

"What do you mean?"

"What I mean is…isn't it odd that our imagery of God is, of all things, human?"

Nanki frowned.

"By subjecting an infinite concept within our finite understanding, we also subject it to our own limitations: God comes with a gender, maybe parts of animals and birds. With human abilities, only exaggerated, like strength and healing. Maybe a few more gimmicky powers here and there. Those too borrowed from what we see and wished as kids to have, like the ability to fly, skim the waters, hear what everyone is thinking, and some grown-up fantasies like turning water to wine."

Damn, is that true? She tried imagining a God, that is actually *beyond* human, and came up empty.

Oh my God, we are so *stupid*, she thought and laughed. River met her laughter with a smile and went on.

"You know why that is? Because we, as humans, are incapable of actual originality. There's nothing original we can really create. Did you know that you can't dream of anyone, not even a bystander, that you haven't seen somewhere in real life?

"The most original art we can create is at best, an imitation of nature—but translated in our own unique way of processing it. You can only write of what is felt—and not a word more. We can only see as far as we have ever seen. You would have to *feel* kindness to truly give it. You would have to honour how life moulded you to solidify your relationship with it.

"Then, maybe, it is that chemistry that is unique, your interaction with the world: how it flows through you, and how it changes as it does, how *you* change as it does.

As we've seen with the evolution of all other relationships, snuffing out individuality for the mirage of the relationship is compromising it by default. Puppeteering corpses doesn't make it a dance.

Caging the storm within only suffocates the life out, and without *your* life, how can there be any experience of it?

"And oh, just like in any relationship, we really need to stop making an example out of one's selflessness and suffering and congratulate their peace instead. That would be a far more loving thing to do, no?

"I guess when you don't even know what contentment looks like and what it makes people capable of, how would you know your system is actually a failure, right?

I don't see how *any* relationship would be any different. Whether it is the one you share with a partner, your work, or *its* to the society it serves.

Or even God."

It was getting late and she gestured for the cheque. The evening was coming to a close. River sat still, "Maybe the edge must not be the place for you. It exaggerates everything—the fears, the will, the courage—the *you*; and turns one inside out. It is not the place one goes to die, its where one goes to remember how to live! To be *alive.* To engage in a dialogue between all of you and all of life."

She smiled, "Yes, yes, a LIVER. I remember…" and after a silent moment of thought, she added "And I've already qualified, so no backsies."

They paid and got up. River looked her straight in the eye and said, "So show me if you're ready. Show me the *most* version of you and show me if you can at least *see* it without panicking and without anxiety, because if you aren't ready—well maybe, you aren't ready."

Whoa, for a liver, he was dead serious.

"Fine then. Don't judge me when I do."

"Don't judge *you* when you do."

They walked out soon after and the cold consumed them all at once. He rode away on his motorbike into the night and she made her way back to her cosy little tent. As she walked away from the circus of lights around the Ganga, it grew pitch dark. She knew only of the rustling of the grass below her feet and the cicadas that grew louder with every step, humming quite madly like children on a sugar high. A couple of minutes later, there at a distance it stood, looming closer.

The light from her tent grew bigger and she ran into its warmth.

A long night lay ahead of her.

***

Nanki was nowhere close to sleep. As soon as she had stepped back into her tent, she had unwrapped her stole, whipped out her notepad, and gotten straight to it.

It seemed from her conversation with River that she would have to write her thoughts all over again, but this story seemed simpler. All it demanded was to be herself, which was probably the easiest thing to do and the hardest thing to start. How could something as simple as that be the answer?

Stop. This time, she was determined. No more double guessing herself. Having unlocked the identity she had been strangling down in chains, her thoughts came, one spilling over the other, just like the coffee she hastily brewed.

It was a fairly simple solution, really. Stupidly simple.

She looked at her bullet points: Manpower, money, stability, visible misery, sustainability.

If Nanki saw this as herself, a brand strategist working on a pro bono project for Dharma Foundation, outside of the Covid timeline, her first obvious objectives would be: to boost its visibility, build credibility and enhance their trust within its target market—a crucial currency for an NGO surviving primarily on voluntary donations.

It would still not cater to the most important flaw in the plan: at least enough stability to ensure sustenance. For a stable flow of human resources, so far in the form of erratic volunteers, they would need employees, for a stable flow of money, they would need income.

Nanki paused. Now that it was on paper, she really couldn't see any other solution.

What social service needed, was *business*.

For this she would need to go beyond marketing, and design a modification for the product itself. There was only one other time she had ever done this. The beverage and a pinch of turmeric. It was the only time she had ever dared to let the story of the brand dictate the product—and it seemed to have worked. The shame started creeping back up again, but this time she was determined to power through, not lifting her eyes from the notepad.

The task at hand would entail:

- A study of their key skills — since they didn't have a single-pointed forte, this would be hard but also allowed her the liberty to choose from their variety of services rendered. These had to be such that they could be leveraged financially. Since they had most notably worked on emergency relief, their skills would presumably include SOS organisation, first-aid training, panic relief. This was enough to build on.
- Then there was a rudimentary interest audit, which was simply talking to the team about what they would be most passionate to pursue. Almost always overlooked, this was as key to sustainability as the availability of tangible resources. What they did was usually a result of their means, but how *well* they did it—that depended how much they liked doing it. The heart of it all was always the epicentre of its actions.
- Market research: a study of those most likely to purchase from them, and then curating the product to suit their needs. This was the oldest marketing practise in the world: Observing what the demand is for in the market and creating its supply. It was just creating a solution for the problems their beneficiaries face.

Nanki looked up. The crudely scribbled plan led to something. Towards furthering her ideation, she was missing a crucial element: feedback from the customer.

She video called River. There was literally nobody else she was left with. The thought almost pinched before she brushed it aside. *Not now.*

This was the first video call she made to him, because she knew from their more elaborate R&D (Research and development) drives that feedback came from more than verbal cues. It came from what they responded to and how they absorbed information.

He picked up on the sixth ring. Nanki knew because she was impatiently counting.

"This is new" he started, his face bemused.

"Hello to you too! You asked me to show you the *most* version of me. This is it. This is what I would do now. What I *may* do.... if it makes sense. Tell me?"

"You're crazy, you know that?" River said, a smile and a frown simultaneously sprouting up on his face.

"Yes and that's besides the point," Nanki had nowhere else to be and yet blurted her plan out in a rush.

After she did so, she added, "Of course, this is all just basis an informal initial chat with Mr Kharbanda. This would be built upon... But I reckon something like an institution of online training on crisis management would work well. They used to run a school—that had started it all, except that these would be paid. A much needed service, sold for its value by people who had field experience to share.

"So short term workshops, maybe a series on life skills like how to stay calm during panic situations, where they share personal experiences, teach basic first-aid, even sustenance rationed cooking, evacuation procedures and such … should have a good market. Especially now, when this generation has just witnessed a crisis and realised first-hand how inadequately we are all prepared for it. It could be something like 'The Art of War' after that book…or like a 'Train for a rainy day' with an umbrella logo…"

She had been brainstorming out loud when she looked up. River hadn't said a word so far. He had the same blank expression he did when he had torn himself away from his book back at the café.

He adjusted his face and cleared his throat.

"Well?" she egged him on. If she had been expecting feedback, he was giving her nothing.

"Your eyes light up when you talk through your work. It's like watching an artist play with their colours. Why would you ever want to lose that?"

Why she would want to lose that? She remembered her fight and now that some steam had been blown off, she buckled under her answer. She flapped her notepad shut. Creative though it was, it had been an entirely futile exercise.

"Because. It takes away from the essence of what they stand for: *Service for service's sake*. To give what one can. Adding money to the mix is to divert their objective to profits, invite stakeholders who are in it for other reasons, like employees who are part of the initiative for the job instead of the intention and build a business on others' fears.

"I dunno, traditionally, religiously or spiritually speaking also, it feels like…*sacrilege*. You don't look for returns from what you give, let alone gains. That makes it selfish, doesn't it? Shouldn't there be somethings that are selfless? I'm at that point where I feel like it doesn't matter that it lights up my eyes, I'd rather light up the *room*… you know?"

She had no idea if this was making any sense. She was having a lot of those moments lately.

River stayed silent a whole minute, his expression unreadable.

"You mentioned something about that at Chai Library too. Let's get into it then. So *you* think that *God* thinks that losing yourself will make you more useful to the world?"

It wasn't a patronising question but a genuine one. She knew that about him by now and liked that most about River. This allowed for full conversations on incomplete thoughts. Not necessarily the destination but the journey. Which eventually was most progressive in actually arriving there.

"The beauty of renunciation? Seems like that may finally be what makes me a better person. It's not that it's not annoying. I just think it's what it is. I think maybe we become...*full* only to realise it isn't nearly enough. Eventually leading us to let go of our delusions. Maybe it is only in selflessness that we find a meaning for ourselves. It is most vain though. That's why I said it. That if I were God, I'd design it differently—because if we are just to receive the world, and let it flow through us, as it may, without any obstruction, what do *we* exist for?

"What, then, is the purpose of *our* being? To whip up dreams, only to let them go in the end? If observing and appreciating is all we're here to do: of what *is*, then what is the point of ever imagining or creating what *can be*? Aren't we supposed to be active participants in our world?"

On this metaphoric bridge she was treading on, just when she thought she was making progress, there was that inexplicable pull backwards and this tug of war felt rather like being caught in a loop.

River started slowly, "What if God turns out to be the *sum* of all things? A God that is dependent on the harmony and well-oiled functioning among all that exists, like you exist within an elaborately designed body—nowhere inside it, and yet permeating through all of it: the blood, the skin, the bones."

It is a most wondrous thing, Nanki thought, to witness someone's faith. She was taken aback by its sheer weight. Fluid but fierce, it was just like River.

She went completely quiet and looked down at her plan.

"But what about doing things from love? It is only normal to *want* to be selfless from love?"

River said, "Ah, love. Oh, I'd hate to think there is a 'normal' definition of it somewhere because 'normal' is just another prejudice. The most all-encompassing one at that. Once we establish an idea as 'normal' we see everything different from it as 'deviant' and that replaces our curiosity with judgement.

Normal love can also look like…self-*full*.

When you are lucky enough to witness that, you realise that 'self-*less*-ness' is such a paltry insult to love. Love is always *more*, no? That's why it is so special. If you've ever loved anyone or anything wholly, you'll know that it could never diminish you. Far from it, in fact, it leaves you enriched from your act of loving and you are never 'lesser' for it.

"It's almost magical, isn't it? How you can be quenched by the watering itself, allowing you the privilege of making the bloom a part of you. So then, what is love but extending your *life* to something outside of it? Expanding beyond the self, enough to include its buoyance within your own river. Love isn't what leaves you parched, it is how you become an ocean.

How can that ever be selfless?—it is *wholesome*.

I really think Karma works the same way too.

It's *ick* how people talk about selflessness and in the next breath of how it would earn them good karma. That's the hook. How many would do good if they knew for sure, it wasn't coming back to them? Goodness is and has always been murky business. But one doesn't usurp Karma points individually like it's a loyalty program in a retail store with a rainbow of happiness at the end. One allows it to happen through us for the *whole* to up its game. The goodness itself is the gift, and the world is richer for it. Just because you created it, doesn't make it any less of a gift. To have more love to go around, leave a heart less heavy and a better environment to thrive in

"I'd rather be imperfect in my authenticity than be perfect on another's plan. It is an act of my faith—I do it as an offering of my prayer.

Seeing sustainability as selfish is like reducing your purpose—and the love that drives it—into a…a…*depreciating* asset.

It must become about 'all of me' build something wholesome with *all* of life. How do I create something unique out of that—now *that* would be a beautiful conversation to have."

Nanki had drifted away into his thoughts, marveling at just how much strength people draw from something as tender as love.

"How exactly would you know the difference between this and that?"

River gave out a boyish laugh.

"By what you look for, and what you see. It isn't righteousness that determines the quality of a relationship, it is *connection*. That is your tether to them. Without that, it's only ever going to be a liability.

If it's causing you to lessen yourself, it's the wrong direction for your love. Arbitrary rules, without a consideration of the individual experience, can only ever assert a transaction, not a relationship. Because can you really *be* connected to something you don't reveal yourself to?

"So *become* you, the *most* you, with a determined detachment to anything that hinders that journey, that's all you're supposed to do. That *is* how Godliness flows through you. You don't *have* to be a tool to God, but that's how you *get* to be magic."

Nanki sat there, stunned, "Self-love, River? That's your answer to an existential crisis? Really?" she laughed. "*The* most abused term on social media, which is what makes it even harder to take seriously, by the way."

River smiled sheepishly. "Not when you say it like *that*. But surely, you would rather have the verb of lovingness than the *idea* of it?" he winked, then added as an afterthought, "besides, commanding one's value can never *decrease* it. Sounds like if you don't, you may be able to spare a couple of hours a month sacrificially. If you do, you allow it to earn your years. Sounds pretty obvious to me, but hey, this is just my opinion..."

Nanki took a long hard look at him, shocked at the dots that he was connecting in front of her like a magician.

It's funny, she thought, how we make rooms out of vastness and imagine holding the key to one and a lock to another—when it is only our illusion of barrier that prohibited entry.

It is also the mind that always had access to any room; for there never were any.

So it *was* Self-Love but it was more. It was *connection*: our sense of *belonging* that determined the quality of our contentment. That's the eternal struggle, the great fight, and the final difference between an average life and a great one. Finding that connection with what we allow to consume us. Even with all the complexities of modernisation, we really are no different from the misfit weed that continues to fight for ground till the day it wilts.

And for a connection to work, its pieces have to fit right. Simply, just right, and that's what makes it perfect. *Therefore,* self-knowledge. It isn't the big picture that solves the puzzle, its observing the structure of the pieces that make it. That is how it can be drawn out of them, although that is neither the objective nor the route. The larger picture is only the illusion that holds the process, keeps the cogs turning—and that is probably its only purpose.

River was right, wasn't he? May we never reduce our love to an unfortunate depreciating asset. May it be fed enough to become fuel. To thrive so as to nourish.

Nanki sat, clutching at her papers, processing. Building friendships, making money, creating contentment, understanding philosophy and morality, marketing and innovation and service, finding a purpose, deepening devotion and through it all, weaving the stories we tell ourselves that tie them all together—everything that makes a life well *lived...*

It's actually pretty *brilliant*, she thought. How it all boils down to the art of relationships—and how the only real way of accessing that knowledge is through unveiling the artistry within oneself.

"So...?" she looked down at her notes. Did she have something here?

"So. Don't discard you. *Use* you. For that, you must find you. You seem to know where to look. Don't stop now."

Not stopping now, Nanki repeated to herself in declaration. Towards that end, she added, "Oh and by the way, on the subject of God, we have been limiting too. We can only see as far as we have ever seen. Why else would we call God a 'He'?"

There. She was going to be aligning with her beliefs now.

He looked up, knowing the night was coming to a close and inhaled deeply "Let's change that, shall we? Here on out, God will forever be they/them."

River ended with a flourish, "And just like that, we're another step closer to understanding 'them', by letting our delusions—a past knowledge fall away…"

They looked at each other and smiled.

"Goodnight, River."

"Goodnight, Nanki."

As she clicked off, finally allowing the night to take her under, *wholesome,* she thought.

It had been a wholesome evening indeed.

15

NANKI woke up knowing what she had to do that day. Maybe it was the restful sleep or the soulful conversations. Or maybe it was because she now actually had the skeleton of a plan.

Whatever it was, she knew that she hadn't quite seen the whole picture yet, only the past. A lot of answers about the future though—those would come from the present.

Mr Kharbanda's *son*. He wasn't involved in the organization—or was he? And why not? What was his vision for its future?

There was only one way she could find out: This meant she had to go rafting.

Oh, what adventures was Rishikesh going to show her?

***

She stood under the scorching sun by eleven am that morning, all set with her sports shoes and her hair tied back in a swishy ponytail. Not that she had to walk any distance, but she felt the need to armour her body. She had loved rafting as a child, but things have a way of seeming like a joyride when you're squished between your parents with the luxury of leaving your fears to them. Alone, now that's a whole different story. There was no one to extricate her body out of this terrifying, chaotic Ganga should it fall into it.

Nanki approached the gushing river, dancing into a rhythm only she knew the notes to, in ripples all her own. As she trudged over the round pebbles adorning the riverbed, a man turned around and

Nanki could have identified him anywhere despite never having met him: Mr Kharbanda' s son had carried forth his stature and his face, minus a couple of decades. He waved out to her.

"Nanki! Hello there. I'm Karan." No handshakes for social distancing.

Nanki reciprocated and smiled. "Hey Karan! Finally we meet. I'm so excited about this!" and looking out at the rapids, bit her lip and added, "I think."

He gave out a laugh that she knew would age just like his fathers, and said, "It's okay if you're scared. You will be more certain once we're in there. So shall we chat over the raft, then?" It was a hypothetical question and he had already started turning towards the black raft tethered to the pier.

Oh God, here we go, Nanki thought.

"We will have another couple on the raft, we are taking a minimal number of people for social distancing. Please sanitise your hands before and after and keep your mask on where possible. Ah—here's your life jacket. Strap it on—this will be a 16-km-long route. We are now at Shiv Puri and will raft down to main Rishikesh within three hours. There are Grade II and Grade III rapids en route, which denotes their difficulty level. This means it is a moderate route but includes a couple of major rapids: like the 'Double Trouble' and the 'Return to Sender'..."

While this was all gibberish to her so far, it did *not* sound pleasant. 'Return to sender?'—What the hell had she signed up for? She strapped herself into her lifejacket, looked up at the vast blue sky, sighed and went in.

***

The water swirled and gushed around her. She was *happy*, the Ganga. Ecstatic, actually.

Wild and free.

Nanki skimmed her fingers through its freezing waters forming a trail of an adoring caress, leaving an imprint of her love for just a moment before the river consumed it whole and flowed eternally on. The raft swayed.

Karan had been briefing the couple so far, who by the looks of them were on their honeymoon.

The woman wore the traditional red bangles and was heavily made up while her husband, also smartly dressed, had his hands firmly glued to hers. It must have been half an hour by the time he carefully scuttled back and settled opposite Nanki, facing her.

"All good so far? We have a rapid coming up in a bit, we'll have to row then."

"All great!" Nanki said, sitting tighter awaiting the storm. "Thanks for arranging this on such short notice!"

"Ah, my pleasure...T'was the least I could do! Besides, isn't it just the perfect weather today?

"Absolutely stunning," Nanki said mindlessly and rushed forth, before she lost her chance, "So when I met your dad—phenomenal work by the way. We are so beyond indebted..."

Somethings put into everyday words sound so *regular,* when they were anything but.

The couple looked over. Nanki mouthed a rough 'Hi' and explained, "You guys must've read about Dharma foundation during lockdown?"

The woman looked to the husband mutely, and the husband nodded vaguely like she was speaking a different language.

"No? Oh okay, they were distributing oxygen cylinders to people's homes, for those that couldn't get a hospital bed..."

"Ah, yes, I think I saw their name on Instagram. Yes, I think I remember now", he looked confused about why she would bring that up and Nanki explained, gesturing towards Karan, "It's theirs! His father started the organization."

She said it like she was introducing a superstar. He responded like she was a child showing off her new toy.

The man looked towards him appreciatively and said, "Wow, that's great bud. Good initiative!"

Karan beamed, partly amused.

Great *initiative*? That's it? No one close to him went through the horror of covid, did they? It hadn't touched him personally just yet. Well, she sighed, good for him. It was easy to tell such people apart now. That's a weird kind of superpower to have earned after one had made it across *that* bridge.

His wife nudged him just then to take pictures of the scene in front, and he diligently whipped out his phone and posed as if on cue, for a series of clearly well practiced selfies.

Pouting and all.

New love makes people stupid, she declared to herself, and turned back to Karan.

He was grinning sheepishly.

"Well, I wouldn't have understood it till I saw it either. And maybe not even then. It's taken me this long to understand why I needed to hunt down the source of this light."

He sat there, smiling quietly. The mountains did too. The river cajoled the rest of the words out, "It was a dark time, wasn't it? Oof, I was dunked so far deep into darkness, that a little sliver of light and I couldn't see *anything* else. It almost forces you to wonder what it would be like to come up for air, to get close to this hope, to be soaked in it… to *become* it."

Had it been any other time, she probably never would have cut this deep. But everyone seemed connected now—bonded by the same grief, the same fears, the same trials of the same time. The married couple seemed exempt from it somehow, which was okay too. She looked at them, blissfully unconcerned with anything outside of themselves, and smiled.

"I honestly just came here chasing butterflies—"

"I don't think so Ma'am," he interrupted her for the first time. He had been looking at her keenly so far and his voice was kind. "I think you came here chasing hope. That isn't an entirely futile pursuit of life. It is probably the bravest." He smiled warmly with an understanding that she felt grateful for.

'Nothing binds people together more than shared pain', Mr Kharbanda's voices echoed in her ears.

"In that case, is it okay if I pick your brain over this, after?"

"Definitely you can! I'm afraid I may not have much to say though. I manage to give very little time to it. But wait back after and we'll chat?"

Nanki nodded.

He held up his hand to stop her from going on.

"Brace yourself, we have Rollercoaster coming up."

He jumped up and announced the rapids on the horizon. They had been instructed on how to row in the beginning and the atmosphere was suddenly charged.

This, here.

Moments that demand you to crawl out of your head make for better plans. The conversation can wait, this moment and this wave will not. Nanki looked at the ominous rapid coming up. That tingling in her toes, that churn in her stomach—*excitement*. Yes, she knew it with certainty now: she really *was* excited.

Nanki held on tight.

Karan gave out a war cry: "Let's start rowing backwards. Full force everyone! Let's welcome Rollercoaster! Har Har Gange!"

Everyone joined into the chorus: "Har Har Gange!!!" Nanki started to row backwards. The husband stood up for a video and had to be sat down for balancing the float. All too suddenly, the waters turned turbulent and there was an uproar of waves, fiercely rushing into each other. The raft swayed dangerously, managing to stay above it all only by the edge of its teeth. As they danced above the waves, rowing with all the force they could muster, the frigid water splashed into the raft and everyone in it looked at each other, now drenched—and giggled.

Once past it, the raft calmed down and resumed a peaceful flow down the stream, only until the next one came along.

***

Karan operated out of a small office. She sat across from his desk, while he stepped out to get her a cutting chai from the stall next door. She looked around her: plastered with photos of rafting, the pale blue walls barely peeked through.

Nanki was drenched but couldn't care less.

Dhruv. She wanted to share it with him. Yell it out, in fact.

Guess who just went rafting!!

Wish you were here! It was INCREDIBLE....

She almost sent it. Almost.

She sighed. All these yells and nowhere to go.

Instead, she wrote to herself:

The habit is the ghost,

Dead, but only almost.

Yep, officially talking to myself now, she thought.

"Here we are!" Karan walked in with two tiny, serrated glasses of tea and placed one in front of her.

"Ah", is all she could manage and held the glass close. Its scalding heat made her extremely conscious of how cold and wet she was.

He sat down and rubbing his hands together, started, "Yes, so. How can I help you?"

She sipped noisily through her teeth, "Thanks for this! I've been a demanding guest, and your family has been most kind."

Karan answered playfully, "Just what we do. We're in the business of kindness, Nanki."

"About that. Just wanted your take on things actually. I think initially I was curious about the scope of work, either like you—or through you. Like I said earlier, I was just sort of inspired to a blinding degree I guess. In comparison to what you guys were doing, everything else seemed to have washed out.

"But I didn't know where to start and that's when I met Mr Kharbanda. Was wondering what kind of contribution you would most benefit from; what was most needed. He said you are flooded with funds and volunteers presently—though I'm sure more are welcome.

"Something he said about sustainability made me think of some sustainable solutions though. I was just not sure if you would be open to looking at regular income streams and running a commercial wing as a parallel unit to your volunteering work."

As she said it, it sounded comical. Who wouldn't want regular income streams? She also simultaneously felt he might judge her for degrading their purpose. Vilifying it; cheapening it. Implying their stupidity almost. As if they couldn't have done that themselves if they so wanted it.

"Of course we would—it depends on how," he sat ahead with his fingers locked in front of him.

"Oh!" she exclaimed, relief washing over her. "I was worried. I wanted to respect that you chose not to…"

Karan put down his glass of cutting chai.

"You think we chose this? Nanki, the intention was—and is—definitely to serve but when that service demands resources and you find most of yours being spent on sourcing those resources—effort and energy that should be spent on the service you set out to extend, it soon starts feeling more like a liability.

"But we didn't know how to restructure because by the time we realised it, our heart was already invested in this living-breathing baby of ours, this beautiful brainchild with all the potential in the world. Before it can reach that potential though, it breaks down and needs to be built up again. It's honestly heart-breaking. But we didn't want to let the people down. Some of them have supported us BECAUSE we're not commercial. Over time, as I saw it, it became like a toxic relationship, that I didn't want my life to become about."

The words immediately took her back to her chat with River and she nodded knowingly.

Karan went on, "And let me tell you something I've realised. We were also commercial—you have to be, to exist in the market. We had to *sell* misery. Not just throw the spotlight on facts, but actually emotionalise it, dress up the *grief* and *sell* it. It wouldn't sell otherwise. Earning charity is its own kind of business.

I don't think it was seen that way. But that's what you have to do, to inspire donations to scale up. When you're out in the field, you realise there's so much more work to be accomplished. You can't feed nine kids on the street and let the tenth go hungry watching everyone else get fed. It creates desperation. To the end customer, all it translates to is a spam call. I'd rather do good work and command its value. But we weren't businessmen. We don't understand this—not well enough to compete anyway."

It's funny, she remembered feeling exactly that when she looked at that man in his PPE kit that morning from her terrace. What could she possibly do? What value could she possibly bring to the table?

"My father was a government servant and is now living on his pension after retirement. Why do you think I didn't do that full time and took up this job? I am so proud of the work we do but dreams need fuel. In an ideal world, they wouldn't, but in an ideal world we also wouldn't need to mend grief. So if we're in the game, whether we like it or not, we might as well learn the rules—that's the only way we can ace them."

Something River had said a while back came back to her now.

'When goodness succeeds, goodness thrives.'

She could appreciate the gravity of that thought only today. Goodness will always be enough but for it to be the absolute rule, the law of the land, it must also win. Why mustn't it? God knows, it deserves to. If only humans upheld its value in the world.

'We really need to stop making an example out of one's selflessness and suffering and congratulate their peace instead. That would be a far more loving thing to do, no?'

Yes, Nanki thought now. As she sat looking at Karan, she realized the consequences of not heeding to it.

We *need* to stop lauding selflessness, she thought fiercely. Not because it isn't noble, but because it *is* unfortunate and glorifying it keeps the doer in more of it. It ties their identity to it, and even at best, even if from love, they only know to stay in and gift this suffrage forward because they were only ever celebrated for that: their failure and exhaustion and drainage. It is only when people come from a long line of suffocation, she realized, to cope, they attach virtue to suffering and honour to pain. The children, who have not known of the pain, just of this learning, internalise it and perpetuate it: with honour, they associate pain; with virtue, they equate repression.

Until someone finally decides that feasting on crumbs doesn't make a hearty meal. Like Karan. In their little acts of self-love, they revolutionize the act of loving itself, and it forever stands changed.

Having seen the cause and now the consequence of Dharma foundation, it finally made sense, and clicked into place: At some point we have to have the courage to own our pain and call it wrong. That is how we begin.

"Okay then," Nanki said, "I may have a plan."

***

It seemed to have become a hybrid. That's what it was. As far as she knew, it didn't have a label exactly—it was just the strengths of two different worlds fusing to form an amalgamous new *thing*.

Nanki smiled thinking over this now with her eyes shut as they sat in yet another meditation session. It had been two weeks since that meeting with Karan and they had been building this new wing for Dharma, page by page, idea upon idea.

This was a much smaller scale than the projects she had been used to. After some rudimentary planning and exciting brainstorming sessions, they had launched 'Kurukshetra', meaning the sacred battlefield—a training institution to cultivate the spirit of a warrior prepared for combat.

The Art of War was the tagline. Mr Kharbanda had loved that one. Nanki had had it incorporated into their website within three days of basic artwork direction and execution. By the seventh day, they had rolled it out on social media after planning schedules for online training workshops with the employees and volunteers.

During the organisation of such logistics, while having to understand their portfolio of work, Nanki was stunned at the experience they had accumulated.

They had so much knowledge, they just didn't understand it's value or it's positioning in the market, if organised right! This is where—and now Nanki could think of it with pride—she shone.

River had been right. As she started feeling this fullness in herself, she could see the value and the route to creating it through her. To having her environment mirror it through her work. *We are how we access the world,* she thought.

The cool Himalayan breeze hugged her and she knew what her purpose had been. To bring herself to the table was all that was required, because nobody had ever charted the exact same route or witnessed her unique landmarks.

It wasn't this or that, it was *everything.* What had to be charted was simply the 'how'. All her questions had been valid, all her experiences led her to here. The past hadn't been a waste, after all. Not the good, not the bad, not the ugly. Not even the shame from that turmeric tip; it was how she knew she had the confidence to do this today. It didn't happen *to* her, it had happened *for* her. To make her uniquely perfect for her imagination from here.

A pinch of turmeric, she thought. That meeting came back to her now and for the first time she didn't feel the need to dig deeper within herself from shame. It was over. Just like that, what had taken hold since that day, finally let go of her and she realised how light it can feel to be free.

The road always forks into two…

Had she not had the courage to take one step ahead of another, even when she couldn't see the way, she would've been heavy with unfortunate luggage for the rest of her years. But because she did, they became opportunities—just stepping-stones, onward her path.

Poison turned to medicine, with a mere shift of perspective and we say we don't have magic.

As she inhaled, she felt it dawning on her. Creating this life, *this* connection with feeling alive—it is divinity, it's God, it's *magic*. To become disconnected with it, is to be disconnected with it all. And without it all, what do we even have?

The fear is if life will still love you back when you do.

Vulnerability then, is the final key. The strength it takes to be fragile enough to *be* and to allow being seen and to build from there. A silent promise to uphold the consequences that flow through us, for that is how the connection with *life* is honoured and strengthened. That's the most important one of all.

She was probably failing meditation again today, but it was more than okay. Today marked one week of having launched Kurukshetra and it had been garnering such a buzz! Since they had been attracting media anyway for their brilliant ongoing work during the pandemic, it had started getting noticed by the press.

As she grew stronger, she knew down to her bones that only she could have made this as robust as it was.

Her phone buzzed. Despite Pihu's huffing reprimand, her eyes flew open to see a text from Mr Kharbanda.

"First milestone achieved. On day 7 of launch, we have officially made bookings worth Rupees One Lakh by hitting our thirty-fourth customer. Thank you Nanki! Transferring Rupees ten thousand to you for your service. Please accept this as a token of our appreciation. You should take this noble work ahead, bete. You are very good at it."

Oh, sweet lord, he had sent her money! She thought she could cry at the gesture. It felt like a report card had been handed to her emblazoned with an A+.

It was in that moment that she felt it for the first time. She was going to be just fine in this life.

16

IT was a windy day. Pihu got out a stack of papers from her mandala-artwork adorned duffel bag. The class had been a good one today and Nanki felt this *knowing* that her time with these meditation sessions amidst these glorious mountains and these pristine beams of sunlight was almost up.

One just knows that sort of stuff, don't they? Want it or not, you can *feel* an experience start to peel away from your life, like wallpaper that's lived its time. Deny it as much as you want, add all the adhesive you need, when it's done, it's just… *done*.

Pihu had an unreadable expression on her face as she started to hand out a leaflet to the five members of class today.

A blank white page with this written in bold:

#IftheWorldCrashesDown.

Not a goodbye.

Nanki looked up for an explanation. Was it just her or was something off about her today?

"This is an initiative by a local Covid hospital here. As we all know, the Kumbh Mela is almost upon us. The number of cases have already been increasing, our hospitals are already full to capacity, and after this…" she fidgeted nervously and paced herself. What was that look in her eyes? Was it fear?

"Well, after this, we don't know what's coming for us. As you all make your way back to your homes before the storm hits, here is what we hope for," she held up a leaflet.

"Find a piece of Rishikesh that means something to you. Make it your own. Write words of love on it and carry them back safely. Identify the people who've meant something to you in this life and let them *know.* Send this to them and send it far and wide.

"Let the language be yours and its expression. Let the words be yours and what you write them on—a pebble from the Ganga or a leaf from a tree or a tissue paper from your favourite cafe.

"Tell them what they mean to you if the world crashes down. Tell them this is not a goodbye. This is just," her voice cracked, "Rishikesh's love letter to the world."

Nanki looked down at her leaflet. Oh, this was morbid.

"You can leave. Come with me!" Nanki felt the urgency to save her.

"And go where? This is home." She smiled through her eyes welling up. That moment right there, blue hair fluttering in the wind, eyes blazing, prepared to go down with the ship—that was how she would always remember her.

Pihu touched her hand warmly, sniffled away the overwhelm and said determinedly, "Don't worry about me. This is not about the fear—it is of courage."

...And Nanki would never, ever forget that.

17

ONE day to Bungy.

Nanki still had a last thing to: a couple of love letters to get through.

The most tender of them all and the yet the toughest task so far. She strolled down to Ram Jhula today in search of her canvas. Pieces of Rishikesh to stow away.

She had already collected a couple of items: A pebble from the bed of the Ganges. Even if it was stolen away from the riverbed, it will always have the river to thank for its smoothened roundedness. This was for Jaya.

A tissue from Chai Library—this one was for herself. The day she went to get it, she had scribbled on it:

"A reminder that life is too short for 'fine', and to never settle for anything less than spectacular. Oh, and also, that if only you bring yourself to a great cup of chai, you will always manage to find the company to go with it.

Just as long as you bring yourself to the table.

With Love,

The version of Me, from Rishikesh."

She had three more to find. In all of her thirty-three—almost thirty-four years now, she had only five love letters to give. And one of those was to herself. *Oh, well.*

She walked along the market with rows of little stores crammed next to each other, selling handicrafts, cheap clothes, jute handbags, strings of Rudraksha beads, dream catchers and so much more than her eyes could absorb.

She was looking for a very specific thing though. She wondered if it would still even be here. As a child, her family would religiously come here for it. A rare fruit, the shape of a scarlet teardrop: The Ram-Phal. Literally translating to the fruit of Lord Ram, it was named after this area because it was only available here. She used to think it was a magical creation of its soil, a tangible realisation of all its myths.

Now as an adult, she wondered how that was even possible, but come to think of it, she had never spotted that fruit anywhere else. She walked up to the end of the street, right up to the Ram Jhula footbridge—and there it was. A woman squatted with a basket bursting with that beautiful Ram-Phal, split in two, bleeding a red she had only ever seen this fruit to have.

She walked up to her and asked for a couple to be bagged and one for now. With a toothy grin and plastic gloves, she cut a fresh one up, salted it with *anardana* masala and handed it to her on a leaf as a plate.

Within its fleshy shell, it held juicy red pearls, almost like a pomegranates. Nanki bit into it eagerly. Tangy, mildly sweet with a delicious sourness! Oh, it was just as she remembered it. She didn't even realise how well she remembered it. All of it came back—the laughter, the togetherness, the love. It's amazing how tastes and smells and places can become triggers—*keys* for a whole bank of memories. In that moment, she realised, it was always a choice: *Happiness*.

She could choose what to do with this access now. Instead of yearning and missing it and making her bitter for what was lost, she would choose fondness and gratitude for what she has had the privilege of having. Everything was a passing station in this journey anyway.

Then she found her third love letter.

The large fig tree with unusually dangly roots right behind the grinning lady selling Ram-Phal. She plucked a leaf, a big broad leaf off of it—a symbol of that epiphany—and that was that!

***

On her way back she had also found a fourth love letter, but first things first.

She opened her mail for the first time since she had come and let the barrage of mails flood in. She wasn't attending to them right now.

She signed the pebble with the hashtag: '#IftheWorldCrashesDown. Not a goodbye.' She clicked a photo of it, attached the image to the email and wrote:

'Dear ~~Jaya~~ WorkMom,

So your work-child is a teenager now. I can only imagine the horror.

Please accept this as my resignation. Your child is only moving out, not moving on. You don't move on from family. Thank you for never giving up on me.

You're right: I do owe you answers. I was only waiting to find them. Please find attached the business plan of my new journey. It has all the details of the project I've been working on and its returns so far. It wasn't a project when I started it but it has shown me new potential—and faith is nothing if not a bet on potential. You taught me that by example. So I'm daring to have faith now.

In a gist, I intend to reach out to add a sustainable income stream to organisations working on charities or donations, market a new commercial line, rebrand and sell for people who need the know-how. Basically what I was doing for the fizzy drink, just for people who need it more. For people needed more. Those doing the work, the world would be richer for. I can handle the project for six months till they take off and charge a ten percent off the profits earned during that time. The details can be worked out. And I've struggled with the service and payment bit. It isn't a service till I've suffered—seemed to have been an operative subconscious thought. Maybe it was survivors guilt.

I've had to rewire myself and question my beliefs around work, money and how it all ties with the idea of self and community and service. While I was walking a path of self-immolation, what I came upon instead was kind of like a crash course on Money EQ—our emotional intelligence around currency.

I've come to realise that the 'selflessness' can be wholesome too, as long as the intention is detached from its reward, but cultivated as fuel by disciplined work. In my proposal, the progress of the work is tracked from impact, not profit but that the impact demands profit is not going to remain a blind spot—it will be seen and it will be attended to with the spirit of service. An empowering, if you will.

Also attaching the picture of a souvenir I'm carrying back for you. Until then, stay safe.

With Love,

from Rishikesh.'

A whoosh and sent.

Nanki brewed herself a cup of coffee. She had two more letters of love to get through.

She wanted to finish the book she had started on her first day here and had a last couple of pages left. She carried it with her along with her beloved cuppa to relish by the Ganges.

Nanki made her way down the familiar path, taking in the crunch of the grass, the view of the mountains, the pure air.

She sat by the roaring river, her feet dunked in its now not-so-freezing water. She spent a couple of hours watching the sun, waves and people pass her by as she flipped through her pages.

Then, without warning her phone buzzed with the notification of an incoming mail.

Nanki sat up straight. It was Jaya.

'Dear Nanki,

It pains me to see you leave. I believed so very much in the dreams I saw for you.

But it is not my place to dream for you.

So let's crack a deal. One last time.

Don't expect me to be entirely happy about this and I wouldn't expect you to change your life decisions based on that. Deal?

In its own way, this loss is its own victory. Because now I know I've raised you better than to be satisfied with being a people pleaser. You're a lot like Nanu, but you're also a little like me.

This mad belief you have, this stubborn optimism about time being worth salvaging, life being more lived, the world standing a chance and the will to chase your happiness: I held the very same faith when I stepped into the advertising world forty years back.

For me to forever think of you as my protégé, it was never the result or the road that I looked for to be the same: it was the spirit.

I did well.

Fly, my child. Consider this as my official acceptance of your resignation.

A social entrepreneur. That should be on your new visiting cards.

Yours,

Work Mom

Nanki's heart swelled with utter joy. Social entrepreneur! So there *was* a label for this. Trust Jaya to always know. Moms always know. She'd have to look into this and study it to deepen her understanding—but what else was all of her life for? Oh, she felt like she could dance!

She felt so…free! A burden off her chest.

One of them anyway: it was time for the next letter of love.

***

On her way from Ram Jhula market, Nanki had picked up a CD of those trippy tantric songs that wafted through all the little streets of Rishikesh. No one used CDs anymore, but oh well, it was symbolic anyway.

She wanted to do this before she left, before her Bungy. When she walked down that yellow bridge from River's video, she wanted to know that she had truly made it through her warpath.

So this would have to be done… and this would have to be done now.

She opened her chat window with Dhruv. It laid vacant, like it had all of this month. He hadn't called once. She had to remind herself that she was the one to have asked for space.

Like an idiot, he gave it. Who *does* that?

She paced the room. This wasn't about her being inexplicably mad. All of the months leading up to this had been about that enough already. This had to come from love. She centred herself with a quick five minute meditation, inhaling and exhaling deeply to gather her thoughts , retracing back to her sense of *connection* with him, before she began:

'If the world crashes down, this is my not-a-Goodbye.

Dear Dhruv,

Did I ever tell you of the exact moment I knew?

My family had already liked you from early on, from when our families would all meet socially. They would tease me about dating you for some reason but I would brush them off. It was obviously not then.

Then that one New Year's eve, when we were all tenting out in that God-forsaken place, getting bored to death, out of the blue, we started talking about stars. I didn't care at all but you wouldn't shut up, you loved the night sky so much. By the end of the night, you had convinced me of their beauty and the magic in their very existence. That's the day I'd reckon we actually became friends, but marriage? It wasn't even then.

A couple of years passed, we dated different people but you stayed my friend. And every time I would look at the night sky, I would think of your love for its stars.

It was when I had gone to Pune for my MBA. It was the first time I was living alone and it terrified me. The night would terrify me and this one time the lights had gone out and the whole area was plunged in darkness. I thought this is it: this is how I die. I closed my eyes and I thought of those stars and out of the blue I asked you to remind me of their beauty to get through the night. And you did.

It wasn't even then, though.

After that, you would check up on me often and we started talking on video calls. You remember that? There were days I had nothing new to say but you would just be on those Skype calls so I was a little less alone. We would both go about our work, dusting, cleaning, cooking, studying with the call running on a stand on our desks. You were my only 3 am friend ever.

It was your being there in the silence—That's when I knew.

And if you're wondering, yes, I always could tell how awkward you were with silence. It was hilarious actually. It still makes me laugh to think of it.

But that's the point, I'm realising.

You really weren't great at it, but you were there.

I'm sorry to have hurt you—I know I have. I'm sorry I wasn't there for you the way you have been for me. You're a way better friend than I am. Always were. It's not an excuse, just a fact.

I'll explain everything else, should you want to listen. I will understand if you don't, though.

Either way, I'm carrying back a souvenir from Rishikesh for you.

Again, if you accept it of course.

Love,

Nanki'

She attached a picture of the CD with the words scribbled on them:

'Let's fill our home with new music. A music of our own.'

And send.

She stretched herself. Her hands and legs and neck. They were tired but had taken on a new life of their own. Change was exciting. To be anchored to just enough constants through the variables, even more so.

She looked at her phone. It was almost eleven pm. She had yet another letter to go and no canvas for it yet.

Nanki looked around her tent with a fondness. Just as she was wrapping up for the day, her phone rang.

Dhruv. Within three minutes of her reaching out.

Oh, the relief. Whatever it was, could be hashed out now, Nanki was sure of it.

As long as he was still around to… *whatever*: listen, talk, yell, fight. He was *here*.

She picked up and went quiet. All the words seemed to have

gone out of her. It was a video call and his groggy face, with his messy hair came on.

For a whole five minutes, they both looked at each and said nothing.

"Hi," he finally relented.

"Hi," she whispered back.

Another few seconds of silence, and then, ever so softly, "I'm still that friend, you know. You just forgot."

"I know," she looked down at her nails. It was hard to meet his eye.

"I'm clearly still not great at it, but I'll always show up Nan. You just stopped asking me to."

If he said another word, she would have to cry and she really didn't want to.

Nanki met his eyes, buried under her apology.

They had been kids back then and that had made it so much easier.

At what point of adulthood, she thought, do we pick up the ridiculous notion that growing up meant not having to ask for help? When growing up is maybe learning how to ask it *better*, sooner, and even more fiercely.

She looked at him, really looked *at* him and realised that growing in strength didn't need to take away from the beauty of vulnerability, that boundaries didn't need to be an electric fence. They could be a loving celebration too to be shared with the ones who deserve the party.

Ones like these.

"Stop seeing through me. I'm here. Is that enough?"

She nodded. It was more than enough. Above and beyond.

"...And what is this crappy music you have bought me?"

Nanki laughed, "Oh, it's the bestttt..."

After a really, really long time, two old friends caught up on their lives till they drifted off to sleep with the call running through the night.

It told the story of a love she was only seeing as it unfolded in front of her: the kind that flowed with the determination of a river, accumulating within its folds all that changed and all that stayed the same—even if it looked like a breaking down to build anew from.

With its essence—a deep friendship—intact through it all.

18

NANKI was shuffling through her room in the early hours of her last day in Rishikesh.

It had come as an epiphany, the canvas for her letter for River.

The book! The very book she had been reading since the first day she arrived in Rishikesh, the one she had picked up from the little library in her campsite reception: the Bhagavad Gita.

The more she thought of it, she wondered how she hadn't thought of it before. She picked up the pen by her bedside table, flipped open to the first blank page of the book and sat down to write:

'Dear River,

If the world crashes down, I'd want you to have this.

This book was written over ten thousand years ago. We hold it sacred and I see why now.

I read it on this trip and here's what I realised: even centuries later, we still ask the same questions of our existence:

Of Identity: Who I am

Of Purpose: Why I am

Of Direction: How to be, so I can be happy.

And in pursuit of those answers, we still always find ourselves standing at the brink of a waging war—only this time, the demons are within. And they're stronger than ever before. Want as you might, you can't turn your chariot and run away from the battlefield. The only way out is through.

Thank you for being the Krishna to my Arjun and helping me walk that one step further.

I am ready. I'm ready for what's to come, I'm ready to meet my fears, I'm ready to see God as they emerge through my faith in letting go of them.

This walk down this path, that bridge—it is of courage.

I am ready for war. Let's see what this edge is about, shall we?

P.S This is not a goodbye. This is an 'until we meet again'.

With Love—and forevermore,

A Liver.'

Yes. This was it—and now it was time.

***

It had been a forty-minute drive up to Mohanchatti—the village within Rishikesh popularised by housing India's highest Bungy. A beautiful winding drive up the mountains through the Lakshman Jhula, the beach camps and the flowing river. Nanki had kept her window rolled down to not miss a single frame of this heavenly landscape.

She had almost lost track of time when with a jolt she saw it: A road sign that announced: 'First View of Bridge: Jumpin Heights—the Bungy People.'

Here it was!!!

That place out of an Instagram handbook of bucket lists. The massive yellow bridge jutting out—the one she remembered River jumping out of. *Whoa*, India's highest Bungy indeed.

Oh, the stories it must hold, she thought as she inhaled sharply.

As she arrived at its reception, she was whisked away to be briefed and her nerves were shooting through the roof. River was probably at the bridge.

After all the safety check ins, it was time! She walked down to the bridge, a quick five minute walk with the cantilever looming closer with every step, threatening…beckoning.

Not for the faint hearted, her.

The glare from the sun was blinding her temporarily when she noticed a tall, rugged and blue-eyed man, walk up to her with a bounce in his feet, and shook her hand: River met her at the foot of the bridge.

Here he was! She instantly felt reassured.

"Finally! Welcome Nanki," his accent was still disconcerting but she knew from experience now that she'd get over it in a jiffy. *What* he had to say always overpowered *how* he said it, exotically distracting though it was.

"River!" she just felt so happy to see him. She took her book out and handed it to him. Her penultimate letter.

He stopped short, curious and flipped it open. When he looked up, she could tell he was touched.

"Not a goodbye," he read aloud, with a smile forming on his face.

"Not a goodbye", she repeated. "One last time, are you sure I can do this?"

"I got you here, didn't I? Trust me to take you through."

It's true, she would trust him with her life. And she literally was about to.

"Everything I've said so far, is only my thoughts and my perspective. I hope you have thought deeply and have arrived here by virtue of your own choosing. Because beyond this point, the journey isn't easy. You will only make it through if it is genuinely *your* will to. I can only promise for it to be worth it."

Nanki nodded.

"And if you have thought over it deeply and arrived here of your choosing, then surrender to the process now and think no more. *This* is that point. The edge. If you decide to walk up to the edge, don't sabotage the experience by your fears. Let the experience take over. The more you think now, the lesser you will be able to act. This is that point where you get out of your own head and just live. Live the moment—it is yours. Less thinking, more feeling.

"Ready?"

Nanki exhaled with a forceful determination. She had decided.

"Take me to the end."

***

The edge is a scary place. In this case, it stood at eighty-three metres from the ground—roughly the equivalent of a twenty-five storeyed building, with her ankles tied together, harnessed to a rubber chord, giving her the first full view of the depth of the fall.

It hit her with the full force of its magnanimity.

Her heart was banging against her chest. River was checking the chords.

She blinked hard as she took in the landscape. A string of mountains jewelled the scene like jagged diamonds. In its midst, lay a wild forest patch. Serene, raw.

The blurry mid-day sun cast a golden hue to everything it touched.

There was a shallow tributary of the Ganga meandering through, gurgling below the cantilever. Just as one would expect her child to be: pristine, naive and free.

Then there was the edge. It brought her the chance to enjoy it all—almost to consume it—if she could only dare to take the jump. But it also showed her the depth she'd have to overcome to do it.

And because that mirrored the battle that she had silently been fighting within her, she could neither bear to stay nor to look away.

"3..." River yelled out his countdown, infusing her with the vigour of his command, "Spread your hands out wide, like the wings of an eagle..." River was right behind her, holding the back of her harness.

Nanki closed her eyes to brace herself.

This was it. This was her moment.

"2..."

Nanki opened her eyes. *Actually*, she decided, she wasn't going to miss it for the world. As she looked straight ahead, determined to surrender even through the jitters, she let herself feel.

It comes as a regular day, the extraordinary one.

Nothing about it is different really—not the weather, not the people, not the life.

It isn't a storm, it isn't a whirlwind, it isn't a beginning, it isn't an end.

Just another day somewhere in the middle but suddenly the sun shines brighter, the wind feels like an adoring caress and the day feels like a lover asking you to *dance*.

And you do.

Nanki looked down the height, forcing herself to breathe.

Just another day, but you're just wholly awake and utterly alive to it.

That's what an extraordinary day looks like.

"1..."

Nanki unclenched her fists and let the fig tree leaf be carried by the wind to her muse.

Her final letter of love. To an eternal love: the mountains of Rishikesh.

It had scribbled in ink:

'You've seeped into me,

Like the salt swirling the depths of the Sea

So I don't even know,

How to let you go,

Because without you, you see,

I'll be empty of me.

—Never a goodbye.'

As it flew away from her, she imagined it persist through all hail and storm: just like her love for them.

She could feel River inch closer. He looked at her while she felt a terrifying calm grip her as she honed in on her goal. She was going to conquer this.

With the fierceness of a warrior opening battle, he whispered—

"JUMP!"

Bungy
At Jumpin Heights
India's First Extreme Adventure Zone